HEXED HISS-TORY

A NINE LIVES MAGIC MYSTERY

DANIELLE GARRETT

ROOTS & WINGS
PRESS

BOOKS BY DANIELLE GARRETT

BEECHWOOD HARBOR MAGIC MYSTERIES

Murder's a Witch

Twice the Witch

Witch Slapped

Witch Way Home

Along Came a Ghost

Lucky Witch

Betwixt: A Beechwood Harbor Collection

One Bad Witch

A Royal Witch

First Place Witch

Sassy Witch

The Witch Is Inn

Men Love Witches

Goodbye's a Witch

BEECHWOOR HARBOR GHOST MYSTERIES

The Ghost Hunter Next Door

Ghosts Gone Wild

When Good Ghosts Get the Blues

Big Ghosts Don't Cry

Diamonds are a Ghost's Best Friend

Ghosts Just Wanna Have Fun

Bad Ghosts Club

Mean Ghosts

SUGAR SHACK WITCH MYSTERIES

Sprinkles and Sea Serpents

Grimoires and Gingerbread

Mermaids and Meringue

Sugar Cookies and Sirens

Hexes and Honey Buns

Leprechauns and Lemon Bars

NINE LIVES MAGIC MYSTERIES

Witchy Whiskers

Hexed Hiss-tory

Cursed Claws

Purr-fect Potions

Furry Fortunes

Talisman Tails

Stray Spells

Mystic Meow

Catnip Charms

Yuletide Yowl

Paw-ful Premonition

Growling Grimoire

MAGIC INN MYSTERIES

Witches in the Kitchen

Fairies in the Foyer

Ghosts in the Garden

HAVEN PARANORMAL ROMANCES

Once Upon a Hallow's Eve

A TOUCH OF MAGIC MYSTERIES

Cupid in a Bottle

Newly Wed and Slightly Dead

Couture and Curses

Wedding Bells and Deadly Spells

*I*t was a place no self-respecting witch and feline familiar should have been. At least, not at half past noon on a Wednesday.

Winterspell's favorite watering hole, Merlin's Well, was one of those bars that was like an old shoe, or a worn-out pair of jeans. Comfortable, if not a little dingy, with a familiar feel that enveloped everyone who walked through its doors. My best friend, Leanna, managed to talk me into coming out to Ladies Night a few times a month, so I guess that made me something of a regular.

But on a weekday afternoon, the only patrons in the place thought of it as some kind of low-rent country club, a retreat for magical folks of a certain kind. Generally, old crusty warlocks and wizards, who enjoyed sitting around day-drinking their way down memory lane.

"Are you sure you want to do this?" Selene's tail twitched, her blue eyes narrowed as she considered the tavern's sign mounted above two thick wooden doors.

"It's not that bad, Selene. Besides, the deputy down at the station house told us Sheriff Templeton is inside."

"When is Sheriff Templeton *not* inside?" The cat's ears went back. "Besides, it's easy for you to blow off a dirty floor. You don't have to walk through there barefooted. Bare*pawed?*"

I rolled my eyes and bent to pick up the cat. Never let it be said I couldn't take a hint. I deposited the feisty feline on my shoulder and pushed open the heavy wooden door.

I paused in the foyer, allowing my eyes to adjust to the relative gloom. The Well's décor tends toward darkly stained wood and old, cracked leather. It wasn't dirty per se as the tavern's owner, a Scotsman named Gerry, saw to its general upkeep, but between the worn floorboards, the furnishings that hadn't been replaced in at least half a century, and the low lighting, it didn't feel like cleanliness was of the utmost importance. In any case, it wasn't the sort of place where you wanted to set your purse on the floor. Not that anyone complained. If anything, the old salts seem to like it a bit dark.

I heard Sheriff Templeton's sandpapery laugh from across the tavern before I could see him. The mustachioed man held court at his customary spot at the corner table, his gaggle of friends hanging on his every word.

"—and that's when this giant shark showed up. I swear, it was like something out of *Jaws*! This big old thing circling us, I could just about hear that music in my head. It brushed up against the boat and sent us sideways. I think Old Mickey about wet himself!"

A round of laughs echoed through the tavern.

"I've never seen him move so fast," the sheriff continued with another guffaw. "Got that motor started up and didn't even bother pulling in the lines. Bob lost his best fiberglass rod to the dang beast."

I stepped up to the table and cleared my throat. Six pairs of weathered eyes swiveled my way, and for a moment, I felt like I must have sprouted wings and horns.

"Excuse me," I said with a pleasant smile, "I don't mean to interrupt your … um … *lunch*—" Though a quick glance revealed there wasn't so much as a crumb of food on the table. Sheriff Templeton and his pals seemed to all be on the same liquid diet. "But I was hoping I could borrow the sheriff for a minute or two."

Templeton sagged back in his chair as he heaved an exasperated sigh. "I don't know what there is to talk about, Cora. I already took your report. We both know this isn't the first time your Aunt Lavender has gone off on some adventure."

I took a moment to tamp down a swell of impatience. "She's not on an adventure, Sheriff."

"Yeah," Selene interjected. "Whatever brain cells you haven't drowned in Pabst Blue Ribbon better listen up. I *saw* a masked intruder carrying Lavender out of her house. She was kidnapped!"

Templeton's eyes rolled to the ceiling. "Oh good grief. The testimony of an elderly cat admittedly under the influence."

My lips pursed. "I hardly think you could say she was under the influence, Sheriff. It was a memory candle, not hallucinogenic drugs."

The sheriff flapped a meaty hand. "All right, fine, but my point is, there's no sign of foul play at her house. No one has called or left a note, asking for a ransom to get her back. And as far as either of you know, she didn't have any enemies who would want to hurt her. So, Cora, what exactly is it you would like me and my deputies to do?"

It was a fair question, I supposed, although perhaps not one meant for me. After all, I wasn't a trained detective. Why was it my job to come up with an idea of what steps to take in a police investigation?

"She's been missing for two months," I continued. "We're all just worried about her, *sir*."

Templeton braced his elbows on the table. "Have you thought about putting up reward money?"

I bit the insides of my cheeks to keep from screaming. How was that his best solution?

"I—I don't know. I suppose I could speak with my mother about it."

Selene's chest vibrated against my shoulder as she released a low growl. "What does the city even pay you for? Does Warden Quinton know you spend your afternoons here, in a dark tavern, slurping up booze and telling old fish tales, while you're supposed to be doing your job?"

That seemed to sober up the grizzled sheriff. He sat up a little straighter in his seat and dropped his elbows off the table's edge. "I'll send my deputies back to Lavender's house to keep looking for clues and see about scraping together some reward money before we open a tip line. How's that?"

"Sounds like the bare minimum," Selene replied.

"It's a start," I quickly interjected. "Thank you."

I turned my back on the sheriff and his pals. Selene fell silent until we stepped back outside into the bright sunlight.

"A third nipple would be more useful than that man," the cat muttered darkly as I placed her on the sidewalk.

I shook my head, unsure of what to do. My muscles were coiled up, ready to spring into action, but there wasn't any to take. Ever since we discovered Aunt Lavender wasn't on one of her treasure hunts, and had instead been abducted, I'd had a tightness in my chest. A rising anxiety that never seemed to fully dissipate. It ebbed slightly when we were busy looking for clues, but after two weeks of searching, we were out of leads.

My lips twisted to one side as I ran through the past weeks of searching. "You'd think more people would be worried about Lavender," I said after a long moment.

"Let's face facts, Cora. Lavender isn't exactly the most well-liked witch in Winterspell. She's not the type of witch who likes to make small talk in line at the market, or bake cookies for the new neighbors. She keeps to herself, and saying she's socially awkward would be something of an under-statement."

I frowned. "Aunt Lavender is eccentric, for sure, but I didn't think people actively disliked her."

"A lot of folks thought she was nuts. Off her rocker. One sandwich short of a picnic. Bats in the belfry—"

"Okay, I get the point, Selene."

The pint-sized gray cat stretched her back into a languid arch, the way only felines can. "And if they didn't think she was crazy, they still found her to be, well, borderline creepy. I mean, what would you think if you caught your neighbor rooting through all the trash bins on a regular basis?"

I blinked. "She'd do that?"

"Oh, yes. Your aunt took that whole 'one man's trash is another man's treasure' thing a little *too* seri-ously," Selene replied with an indignant sniff. "She didn't mind getting her hands dirty if she thought she might find some kind of trinket or bauble for her never-ending collection."

"Yikes." I exhaled slowly as I scanned the street. Summer had ended and Winterspell was in some-thing of a slump as the seasons shifted. In the summertime, the magical town was packed with tourists and out-of-towners who came to vacation or visit from the non-magical world.

Things would pick up again in the winter, when the snow started falling and the mountains surrounding the picturesque town would open for winter sports. For now though, things were quiet and peaceful. It was often my favorite time of year, as my candle shop was a little less busy and I could cut out early to soak up the last of the season's longer days on the lake. However, right now, even out on the lake, my mind was too loud. My thoughts too rapid. I didn't think I would be able to properly unwind until we found Lavender and brought her home again.

"Well, law enforcement isn't getting any closer to finding her." I looked over my shoulder at Merlin's Well. "Sheriff Templeton has clearly already written Lavender off. I guess he figures she'll show up on her own and isn't too concerned if she doesn't."

"Ah, we don't need him." Selene's ears went back. "Sheriff Templeton is a bumbling idiot on the best of days. He's not a trained detective. Winterspell doesn't even have one of those."

She was right. The magical community was guarded by enchantments and highly trained sentries. No one from the outside world could get in save via a single road leading in and out of town. Life in Winterspell could get busy in the peak tourist seasons, but overall it was a safe, quiet little community. The kind where everyone loosely knows everyone else. The residents trust each other, and crime, beyond stupid teenager antics, is basically nonexistent.

Or, at least, it used to be.

"You really think we can find Lavender, Selene?"

The cat swished her tail. "Why not? We solved the last case on our own, didn't we? If we'd left that matter to Templeton, your boyfriend would be rotting away in some prison cell waiting for his trial date."

"He's not my boyfriend," I corrected the cat, though I couldn't help but smile a little. "And we didn't do it all on our own. We had Clint's help, too."

"Yeah, yeah, he was great for cowering in the corner while we did all the hard work. My point is, we've got this."

I arched a brow. "Okay then, master detective, what's our next step? Because I was under the assumption we were stumped, hence the need to go and talk to the sheriff."

Selene lapsed into silence. I have learned to treasure such times.

"Well, we still haven't finished going through the rest of Lavender's house," she finally said.

I groaned in exasperation. "Yeah, and there's a reason for that. We can barely keep track of our own rear ends in there."

When it came to Aunt Lavender, the term *hoarder* might not be strong enough. Her bungalow was stuffed to the brim with odds and ends, with only a narrow passageway leading to the different rooms. Selene and I had been working our way through it, but so far, we hadn't found anything helpful, and the sheer work of going through everything was beyond exhausting.

"I think our best bet is the guest room," Selene said, already marching down the sidewalk.

"We can't even get the door open, and the window is painted shut. Seriously, when was the last time Lavender went in there? You used to be her familiar and even *you* don't know how she managed to get herself out of there."

Selene kept walking, her tail swishing with every other step. "We'll figure something out. For all we know, she's put some kind of spell on it."

"Okay, but if we don't even know what the spell is, how are we supposed to break it and get inside?" I asked, jogging a few paces to catch up.

"I can't think of a solution with all of your yapping. Just drive us there. I'll figure out a way to get inside."

I opened my mouth to argue, but then closed it. As annoying and brash as Selene could be, I had to constantly remind myself that she was just as worried—maybe even more so—as I was about Lavender. She wasn't good at showing her true emotions, and tended to paint everything with the angry brush.

Wordlessly, we got into my car and I drove us to Lavender's house on the other side of town. From the outside, you'd never know that Lavender has been missing for two months. After numerous complaints from the neighbors and city council, I'd roped my brother, Evan, into coming over and fixing the place up. Ever since, he'd been coming over weekly to cut the grass, pull weeds, and trim down the hedges. He'd even tended to her herb garden.

Of course, once you open the front door, that semblance of order goes right out the window. I've never seen what her house actually looks like behind the stacks of accumulated junk she has. She bought the house before Evan and I were even born, and by the time I was old enough to start remembering things, it already looked the way it does now.

Selene and I had slowly been working room by room, but we didn't dare to get rid of anything. So it was something like a giant Tetris puzzle. We had to go through stacks of things, only to create new stacks in a slightly smaller space, to clear the next row of items to process. Most of it was junk. Hundreds—maybe thousands—of books, old magazines, records, and odd trinkets. She used empty boxes from pantry staples to store smaller items like marbles, crystals, and stones. Near the foyer there was a stack of Velveeta cheese boxes, and at first, I'd thought she just hadn't bothering tossing them out, only to find that instead they were all full of small fossils, beads from broken necklaces, and precious stones. If I didn't know better, I would think that at some point she'd planned to start a jewelry-making business, but upon the discovery, Selene had informed me that each item held some quantity of magic, and Lavender was holding on to them until she could uncover what the exact nature of said magic was.

According to Selene, my aunt Lavender was almost something of a one-woman magical bomb squad. She had her more eccentric quests, chasing after rare things like the horn of the first known unicorn, or Merlin's training wand, or the cursed dagger that killed some famed dwarf king five hundred years ago. That sort of thing. But more often than not, she was after smaller, more mundane-seeming trophies. Rumors would swirl about a cursed ring, or a hexed book, and away she would go. Off to track it down in hopes of keeping it from falling into the wrong hands. Anytime she ran across something with magical properties—be it a set of Russian nesting dolls or a cuckoo clock—she'd purchase it and bring it back to her bungalow for safekeeping.

The problem was, she enjoyed the hunt far more than she liked unraveling magical secrets embedded in enchanted or cursed items. That kind of work took precision and patience. And focus. Selene told me that Lavender generally only did that part when she needed to sell something. She didn't have a conventional job, so whenever her funds ran low, she would round up items she was willing to part with, dispel the charms or break the curses, and then sell the items at a flea market she frequented in the non-magical world.

Judging by the state of her house, she hadn't needed to sell anything for quite some time.

Selene moved more easily through the house than I did, and reached the door to the guest room first. She ran one paw down the grain in the wood, her eyes falling closed. I stopped in the sliver of hallway and waited, trying to be quiet as she listened.

When her eyes opened, she shifted them my way.

"Well?" I asked. "Anything?"

"I'd say it's definitely enchanted, but I don't know how ... or why." Selene sat down and considered the door again, her head slightly tilted to one side. "I don't even know when she did this, or how I failed to notice."

The cat fell silent and my heart wrenched in my chest. "You did your best to help her. I'm sure she just forgot to tell you. Got distracted, or something."

Selene didn't say anything in reply. She just kept staring up at the door.

I clasped my hands together in front of me and wrung my fingers together nervously. "We could get the axe from the shed out back," I suggested.

Selene's eyes snapped to mine. "Are you insane?

If this door has been spelled shut, all you'll manage to do with an axe is slice that pretty face of yours clean off. And I am *not* cleaning up that kind of mess."

I reached up and brushed my fingertips across my nose. "Right."

"Just let me think. Go see if we have any more snacks in the fridge," the cat groused, shifting her attention back to the door.

I didn't love that my usefulness was being boiled down to the official snack-fetcher, but I did as she asked, and wound my way to the other end of the house to the kitchen. It was the cleanest of the rooms, as we'd been using the dining table as our main workspace—once we'd unearthed it, that is. The kitchen counters were cleared off as well, and after removing all of the spoiled food in the fridge, I'd given it a good scrubbing and then stocked it with some provisions to get us through the long days of cleaning and searching.

Selene was beyond picky when it came to her food, but in the nearly two months since she'd arrived on my doorstep, informing me she was now my familiar, I'd learned a few of her favorites and managed to keep them on hand—despite my bank account's protests. The cat had expensive taste. I was just about to open a new canister of chef-prepared, all-natural, organic, no-preservatives, free-range cat chow, when Selene's voice called out from down the hall.

"Cora!" The cat's voice bounced around as she raced to the kitchen. "Cora! It's open!"

I abandoned the cat food and hurried to meet her in the hall. "What kind of spell was it?"

Selene had a near infinite amount of magical knowledge, but seeing as she was a cat, her own magical range was somewhat limited.

The cat rolled her eyes. "Another one of her riddles. I swear, that woman must have been a sphinx in another lifetime."

"How did you reveal the clue?"

Selene padded back to the door, which was now slightly ajar. A series of green runes glowed in the wood casing around the doorway, though the light appeared to be fading. "I used a Third Eye spell, to uncover that which has been concealed, and there they were." She used the tip of her tail to gesture at the runes.

"You can read those?" I asked, leaning in closer to try and study them before they disappeared back into the wood.

"Of course! What do you take me for, some kind

of dunce?" Selene tossed her head and slithered into the room. "Honestly, Cora, sometimes I wonder about you."

"Right back atcha," I muttered, pushing the door open a little wider to follow her.

2

"*H*ow could there possibly be *more* books?"

Selene scoffed. "Oh, Cora. There can always be more books."

As a bookworm myself, I could appreciate the sentiment, but Aunt Lavender's guest room looked like someone had taken an entire library and shoved it into a twelve-by-twelve room. The closet doors had been removed somewhere along the way, and the entirety of the reach-in space was stacked, spines out, from floor to ceiling with leather-bound tomes. A row of bookcases spanned the opposite wall, with each shelf packed with scrolls, books, and piles of paper bound with string. Overflowing cardboard boxes were shoved into any other available space, though the books spilling out from them had a layer of dust, suggesting they hadn't been touched in some time.

The window straight across from the doorway was not only painted shut, as we'd found when we tried to get in through the outside, but was also blocked by an enormous piece of poster board mounted along the wall, covering all but a tiny sliver of the glass panes. A bit of natural light flowed in from the top edge, but not enough to provide ample lighting for research or reading. Along the poster board were bits and scraps of paper, arranged in columns.

"What is all of this?" I asked, still marveling at the barely controlled chaos.

"Lavender calls it her research library. I organized it at one point," Selene said before sneezing in the dusty air. "Darn it! Every time I got it looking halfway decent, Lavender would come through like a freaking hurricane and put it back 'her way.' So irritating. Eventually I gave up."

"I don't even know where to start," I confessed, before taking a few steps deeper into the room. The floor was relatively clear, save for stacks of more books. A desk sat underneath the posterboard, and was also surprisingly functional. An antique lamp sat in one corner, and an assortment of pens were corralled into a cup on the opposite corner.

"If Lavender's abduction has something to do with one of her zany research projects, we won't make any progress until we figure out exactly what she was looking into," Selene said as she took a turn about the room, scanning the books as she went. "We've found no clues anywhere else in this monstrosity of a home."

"Did you ever tell Lavender how you felt about the mess and clutter?"

Selene laughed. "Of course. Cora, do I strike you as the type to suffer in silence?"

"Touché," I mumbled. At least she was self-aware enough to know what a pain in the rear she was. That had to count for something.

"Lavender always promised to purge. To do some spring cleaning, hold a yard sale, pare down." Selene paused and shook her head. "She just doesn't have it in her. So, I spent a lot of time outside or away from the house. It's not like she's a terribly good conversationalist. Most of the time I wondered if she'd even noticed I was gone."

I frowned. "I'm sorry. That couldn't have been easy."

Selene's whiskers twitched. "Well, let's get her back, and then I'll let you take a crack at getting her to clean this place up."

Nodding, I turned to the bookcases and picked up one of the scrolls, only to knock over an entire stack. Muttering a string of curses, I bent over and picked them up from the floor.

Selene jumped up onto the desk and peered at the posterboard. "Looks like she was putting together a list of things to sell."

"More?" I asked, turning away from the scrolls quickly before I managed to make another mess. "We already found one stack of receipts. I thought you said she doesn't usually sell more than a few things at once."

"Normally, that's true. She must have been planning a trip, just as I suspected." Selene's tail swished through the air with an agitated flick. "She'd been secretive, more than usual. Keeping this room closed off, barely speaking more than the usual pleasantries each day, closing books when I'd walk into the room."

My brow furrowed. "But why hide something

from you? You were her familiar." A little pang of guilt nipped into me at the past tense. I still wasn't sure how my aunt would take it when she found out Selene had abandoned her and chosen to bond with me instead. Normally, she wouldn't have come to me until after my aunt's death, as she served as a Hearth family familiar, moving from one generation to the next. However, as Selene had explained it to me, Lavender's abandonment of her had created extenuating circumstances and she'd decided to ditch the rules. We just weren't sure what the consequences would be.

"She must have thought I wouldn't approve," Selene replied. "Lavender sometimes had crackpot ideas, and I was the only one around to tell her she was being ridiculous. Besides her lack of housekeeping skills, it was the thing we quarreled about the most."

"So, then, can we work backwards from there? What were some of the quests you shot down over the years? Are any of them ones she might have circled back to? Or had a hard time letting go?"

Selene canted her head to one side, still looking up at the posterboard, studying Lavender's scrawling handwriting. "It's hard to say. I thought most of her ideas were far-fetched."

I rolled my eyes. Generally speaking, a witch's familiar was meant to be a helper, a confidant, a cheerleader. Selene had somehow missed all of those components. She was helpful, at times, but only if the price was high enough. As far as being a confidant, I trusted her, but only to a degree. I cringed every time my mom or brother brought out an embarrassing story from my childhood at our bi-weekly family dinners, because I know Selene was sitting there, absorbing it like a sponge, and would have no qualms about using it at a later date for maximum humiliation.

As for cheerleading … let's just say, if given enough time, she could probably make Oscar the Grouch cry.

"None of her recent clients knew anything about her plans either," I continued. "But remember, some of them said she seemed edgy. Kind of nervous. I always imagine Aunt Lavender charging in, full steam ahead, but were there any quests or treasures that scared her?"

Selene considered the question for a moment, then shook her head. "No. Lavender knew how to get herself out of a pickle, if need be." The cat fell silent for a moment, then added, "Until now, at least."

My lips pressed together as a wave of emotions rolled over me. My hands began to twitch as I looked around the room. "Well, I guess putting it off is no use. We might as well get started. I'll start looking through these books—they seem to be the ones she read most recently since they're beside the desk. Maybe you can work on organizing the notes."

"Organize them how?"

"Alphabetically by subject? Or maybe chronologically might be better?" I sighed. "I don't know, Selene. You said you tried to organize this once before, why not use the same method?"

"Alphabetically by subject it is."

Sparks of magic pinged off the posterboard as Selene flicked her tail, directing each *zing* of pink sparks to do her bidding. Soon, all of the notes that had been affixed to the board sat in front of her paws. For all her complaining about not having opposable thumbs, she could get things done when she wanted.

I sat down in the chair and began working through the stack of books. Lavender had left more notes jammed into the spines of some of them, and I carefully read each one as I flipped through the various tomes. Although, after the first five books, I was left wondering if it might be easier to find things that Lavender *didn't* research. She had notes covering all different sorts of subjects. The fountain of youth. The Holy Grail. The Ark of the Covenant. The Sword of Damascus. The Loch Ness Monster. Bigfoot. It seemed like if there were any subject, any mystery, no matter how arcane or unlikely, Lavender had at least thought about researching it—at least seriously enough to procure half a dozen books on the topic.

In many cases, she'd out and out mounted an expedition. I couldn't follow her notes, as they meandered all over the place. It seemed she didn't care much for chronological order, or any kind of order other than what she held in her head.

I got the volumes in order, but found nothing specific enough to help, and decided to go back to the scrolls. This was much harder, since she didn't bother with titles. I had to unfurl and read each and every one by hand. A lot of the time, Lavender would flip the scroll over and start an entirely new subject, meaning I had to go over them all twice.

Lavender's handwriting was … well, unique to say the least. I can read cursive, but I'm used to people sticking to either cursive or printed letters, but Lavender didn't seem fenced in by those rules, switching back and forth, even in a single word.

Many times I would find a number at the top of the scrolls that corresponded to another on a different scroll. This meant that organizing the scrolls by subject proved next to impossible.

I tried to separate the scrolls by how likely they were to make people money. I was going over the purported map to El Dorado, the lost city of gold, when I heard Lavender's phone ring.

Selene and I froze. No one had called Lavender in some time. On the second ring I bolted out of the guest room and angled down the narrow hallways formed by Lavender's stacked treasures.

"Where's the phone?" I blurted, throwing aside a stack of *National Geographic* magazines.

"It's in the living room."

"Surprisingly, that's not super helpful right now," I said through gritted teeth, before falling silent in time to hear the next trill. The sound echoed strangely off her piled treasures. I narrowed it down to a corner of the front room that Lavender had filled with different sized animal skulls, a mounted barn owl, and a murky jar that Selene said contained a preserved dragon heart.

"I think it's in here, somewhere," I shouted, before muttering to myself as I stepped over a terrarium filled with more animal skulls. "Why she calls this a living room when there's nothing *living* in it I'll never know—wait, there it is!"

Selene trotted over to a cord thrusting out of a mass of spooled yarn. I padded over, but by then Lavender's answering machine had picked up. The boxy thing was something of a fossil itself, a testament to another era.

"Lavender, this is Sal," said a gritty voice. "I know you've been dodging my calls. And I know why, too. I know what you did, and I'm about ready to call Warden Quinton and have her personally stop by and pay you a visit. Call me back the moment you get this message."

The call ended, and I looked to Selene with confusion. "Who the heck is Sal, and what's he talking about? What has Aunt Lavender gotten herself into this time?"

The cat swished her tail. "Sal is short for Salvatore. Salvatore Greco."

"The name sounds familiar," I pursed my lips thoughtfully. "I can't put a face to the name, though."

"He's a trustee for the International Magical Library Society," Selene said with an edge of reverence I'd never heard her use before, which in and of itself was fascinating.

"Not only that, but he serves as an archivist for

the Arcane Council," she continued. "If they need to track down some obscure magical law or code, they call Sal. He's done almost as much research as Lavender has, and he's more organized to boot. Not that it takes much." The cat gave the living room a disdainful sniff.

Suspicion brewed in the back of my mind. "So, what does any of this have to do with Lavender? Are they old friends, or something?"

"They go way back, before my time with Lavender. All I know is she sees him every couple of months, more often if she's really stumped."

"Why's that?" I asked, still not quite piecing it all together.

"Look, no matter how much you gussy it up by calling him a trustee or an archivist, it all boils down to the fact that Sal is a librarian. He has access to the entire Arcane Council and their research library, and with his credentials, if there's a book he wants, he can get it. No questions asked."

My brow furrowed. "So, she borrowed books from him?"

"Sal's stingy. He doesn't let anyone *borrow* books. She'd go and use his personal library when she was researching something, but if she wanted to take something home, she'd have to cough up a pretty penny. Sal has something of a side hustle, as the kids say these days."

"It sounds to me like they are more than just acquaintances, if he allowed her to use his personal library. That sounds more like they're friends." I glanced at the answering machine. "Or *were*, anyway. He didn't sound too friendly just now."

"Yeah, I guess so. As much as Lavender is friends with anyone. I'd say it's more business than anything else."

"Hmm. Well, in any case, it sounds like he's looking for Aunt Lavender too. Maybe he knows something we don't know?" I only waited for a few more moments before motioning for Selene to follow. "Come on. Let's go."

"Where are we going?"

"To see Salvatore Greco, of course."

Selene sat back on her haunches. "One does not simply go and see a man like Salvatore Greco."

I raised an eyebrow at the cat. "Why not? Does his house have a moat around it or something?"

"Of course not. Don't be ridiculous."

"I'm assuming you've met him, so he'll know I'm not lying when I tell him who I am. We're looking for Lavender, and he's looking for Lavender … our interests overlap."

"All right, but afterward, we're hitting the fish market. It's your day off, and there is no excuse for missing them before they close this time."

"Yeah, yeah, yeah," I said, fishing my keyring from the back pocket of my jeans.

3

We headed back out into the sun and fresh air, a welcome change from the dusty, claustrophobic confines of Aunt Lavender's house. I looked down at the smoky gray cat by my side and stopped short. "He does live here in Winterspell, doesn't he?"

My nervous energy had propelled me out the front door before I fully thought through my plan. Lavender traveled all over the place. It was more than possible that Salvatore lived in some other magical town, or maybe even in the non-magical world.

Selene didn't miss a step. "Oh yeah, he's got this monstrosity of a house on the water. Not too far from your oh so *charming* future mother-in-law's place, come to think of it."

I started to object, but quickly decided to save my breath. Selene loved nothing more than baiting me into an argument over something silly. She had petty down to an art form.

"He's probably got about an acre, most of it gardens, with statues and oddly shaped topiaries. A big greenhouse, though he doesn't strike me as much of a gardener." Selene continued at a brisk pace, down the front steps of Lavender's bungalow, and then to wait not-so-patiently at the passenger-side door of my car. "Honestly, you're something of a book nerd. You should have become an archivist. Maybe then you could afford something nicer than the shack you live in."

I frowned as I jammed my thumb against the button on my key fob. "Shack?"

"Did I stutter?"

Sighing, I dropped into the driver's seat, reached over and pushed open the passenger door, and then closed my own. A gust of air magic was all it took to shut it behind the finicky feline, and within a minute, we were backing down the short driveway.

"Did I mention that Salvatore has one of those fancy infinity pools?" Selene asked, peering over at me from across the center console. "Maybe you should think about getting a water feature. It might class up the place."

"Oh, yeah? Well, there's always that pothole in the driveway that fills up when it rains," I pointed out with a sly grin.

"Oh, yes, silly me. The picture of refinement."

"Listen, I know you want your own chambers, but it's just not going to happen, Selene. I like my house."

The cat twitched her whiskers with a distasteful glower.

"Besides, I don't need a pool. The lake is within walking distance of my so-called *shack*, thank you very much."

"Uh-huh." Selene didn't look convinced. I didn't know why she even cared; it wasn't like she would be running out to use the pool even if I did have one. Sometimes she liked to fuss just to fuss.

My phone rang when I pulled out onto the street. I'd slipped it into the mount affixed to the vent fins nearest the steering wheel and could easily see it was Clint calling. With a slight frown, I tapped the red button and sent the call to voicemail before shifting my gaze back to the road in time to stop at a four-way intersection a few houses down from Lavender's bungalow.

Selene squinted at the screen. Being nosy was her full-time job as far as I could tell. She certainly didn't pull her weight at Wicked Wicks. "Clint called?"

"Yes."

"Aren't you going to call him back?"

"Not this minute, no."

"Why not?"

I gestured at the intersection ahead of us. "We're busy right now, remember?"

I didn't have an exact address, but if Salvatore's house was near Clint's mother's estate, I had a general idea of where to go. With a sigh, I hit the blinker, then rolled through and made a right turn.

Selene placed her paws on the center console and stared up at me. "What's the deal? Is something going on with you two?"

I shot her a quick frown before returning my gaze to the road ahead. "Why are you being so nosy? Didn't you ever hear what happens to curious cats?"

"Ha! Even if that sentiment were true, you forget that I can't die. I may be on my ninth life, but I—"

"Snatched the thread from the Fates' hands, yadda, yadda. I know," I interrupted, rolling my fingers through the air. "You've mentioned it once or twice."

Selene soured and sat back on her haunches. She refused to travel in a carrier or use any kind of safety seat meant for pets. I'd made the suggestion shortly after she'd moved in with me, and spent the next week convinced she was going to claw my eyes out in my sleep just for daring to recommend such a thing.

"You're deflecting," the feline replied. "You don't want to talk to Clint, and I want to know why."

"Maybe I just don't want to talk to him in front of your snarky self. It's not like you have anything positive or uplifting to say."

"Nah, I don't buy that either. Is he into something weird? Did he hit you up in the middle of the night for feet pics?"

I gaped at the cat. "Selene!"

"Oh, wait, no, I know. He's a nerd, right? He wants you to do dress up like Princess Leah in that golden bikini thing, with the space buns—"

"I'm worried he doesn't like me, okay!" I blurted. My angry retort hung in the air for a long moment.

Selene canted her head to one side, stunned into silence. "That's ridiculous. He's like a little lost puppy around you. Has been since the night he showed up in your shop. Remember? He almost bought his mother all of those erotic candles." She grinned at the memory. "Absolutely hopeless."

I exhaled. "I'm worried that he's only using me as an excuse to get away from his current living situation. It can't be easy, providing hospice care for your parent, watching them slowly fade before your eyes …"

"He was falling all over himself to be around you before he even knew about his mother's condition," Selene pointed out.

I'd never expected her to take on the voice of the angel on my shoulder, but I had to admit, she had a point.

"I guess so," I sighed. "But that's why he's staying in Winterspell. If not for his mother's condition, he would have left shortly after his brother's murder investigation concluded, and I'd probably have never seen him again."

"You don't know that."

We drove over a babbling brook and headed out of Winterspell proper. The pines sighed in the stiff breeze coming off the mountains, mellowing out the heat of the sun. It was a beautiful day, too beautiful to be discussing my relationship woes.

"All I'm saying is that for the past two weeks, the

only times we've gotten together, he's fresh off dealing with his mother and stressed out. I don't begrudge him that, I can only imagine how difficult and draining it all must be, but … I want him to want to hang out with me because he likes me, not because it's convenient."

"If anything, he should be worried about you," Selene countered. "For all he knows you're just with him to get at that fat bank account he keeps referencing."

I snorted. "You would think that way, wouldn't you? The thing is, I'm afraid that the only thing keeping Clint in town is his mother. And once she passes … won't he just go back to his big city office?"

"Perhaps. Have you asked him?"

"Stars, no. That's the kind of talk you have when things are getting serious." I laughed helplessly. "And I guess I'm afraid of things getting serious, because I'm afraid of him leaving me and this small-town life behind."

"He's not Roger, you know," Selene said.

"What?"

"He's not Roger, your ex-husband. There's no indication he'll behave the same way."

Something burned in my chest and I quickly

swallowed. "It's fine. I'm sure it will all work out how it's meant to."

I expected Selene to push it, but she fell silent, too, only beginning to speak again when we neared our destination. She told me where to turn, and within a few more minutes, we were on a blacktop road, winding through the pine trees in a gentle meandering slope. I remarked to myself it would be quite a nice hike, with scenic views of the mountains.

Salvatore's manor house squatted firmly on the cusp between elegance and hardy safari base camp. It greatly resembled a mountain resort lodge from the seventies, in all the right ways. I parked in the hairpin drive separating the main manor house from the warehouse-sized garage and adjacent green-house. The door to the garage stood partially open, revealing a cascade of highly glossed vintage cars. It seemed books weren't the only thing the man collected.

I walked up the steps to his porch and used the brass knocker shaped like a lion to announce our arrival. I halfway expected a maid or assistant to answer the door. Instead, a great, shaggy-bearded man with a balding pate and a smoking jacket flung the door open.

His dark, glittering gaze scanned me quickly, then dropped to the cat sitting politely at my ankles. He snorted. "I see. Lavender has taken to sending proxies in her stead? Well, you can tell her it won't work. I know she stole the book, and there is no sum she can offer to entice me to sell it to her. So, as I said in my multitude of messages, she can either return it, or she can await a visit from the Warden."

He started to close the door, and I put my foot in the way. "Wait, Mr. Greco, please, we need to speak with you."

"Is the old gal scared of me? Afraid to come and face up to what she's done in person? Hmm? What an insult to send a novice witch and a scraggly old cat in her stead."

"Who's scraggly?" Selene snapped.

"Please calm down, Mr. Greco. My name is Cora Hearth. I'm Lavender's niece. I'm afraid my aunt has been taken."

Salvatore's mouth closed for a moment. "Taken? By whom?"

"We don't know, sir. We were searching her house for clues when we heard your phone message."

He chewed that over carefully for a moment, and then stood to the side and held the door open.

"Please, come inside. And call me Sal. Hearing myself referred to as Mr. Greco makes me feel as though I'm in court or something."

Salvatore led us through his parlor and up a flight of elegantly shallow marble stairs to the second floor. Expensive wood paneling engraved with woodland scenes lined the corridor, interspersed with oil paintings of pastoral settings.

"We can speak in my study comfortably," he said, opening the door and gesturing for us to proceed before him. I walked inside, and noticed all the trappings I'd expected. Obligatory wild animal heads on the wall? Check. Giant granite hearth with a roaring fire? Check. Full bar with shelves filled with liquor? Check.

Salvatore noticed me looking at the bar. "Would you like a drink?"

"No, thank you." I looked at the shelf, noticing many of the bottles were unopened. "Though it does look like you have good taste."

Sal smiled sadly. "Thank you. Although, sadly, I can no longer partake of any of it. My doctor has been quite adamant that even the occasional drink could lead to severe consequences."

"Then why do you have so much booze?" Selene blurted.

"Selene …"

"It's fine. I'm not offended. People often don't know what to buy a rich man—what to get for the man who has everything on his birthday—it seems the default is pricey liquor."

The study was the epitome of organization. A polar opposite of Lavender's place. Through an archway, I could see Salvatore's personal library. I couldn't keep the impressed look off my face as I beheld its many rows of shelves and books stacked to the ceiling.

"I see you've noticed my pride and joy." Salvatore chuckled.

"I understand you let my aunt peruse your private library."

"Oh yes, on many occasions. Even now, there's a couple of university students in there somewhere, doing research." He chuckled. "I do so love to help the younger generation."

"Geez, maybe we should get him to help us organize Lavender's place," Selene muttered.

"Now," Salvatore said, seating himself behind his desk, where he obviously felt more comfortable. "Tell me of your Aunt Lavender. She's been taken, you say? What's led you to that conclusion?"

I pursed my lips in thought, wondering how

much I should tell Salvatore. I wasn't entirely sure we could trust him. "Selene witnessed Lavender being taken by a masked assailant. This was almost two months ago, and no one has seen or heard from her since."

"That's simply awful." His brow furrowed in confusion. "It seems like it was only a few days ago that she was here, but I suppose you're right. It must have been mid-July, a warm day."

"Do you remember what she was looking into?" I asked. "We think her research might have had something to do with her abduction."

"She was looking for the Death Mask of Pharaoh Hori the III. A cursed item, to be sure. I let her peruse the *Odyssey of Obin Amorath* in her search."

My brow furrowed. "What's that?"

"Oh good grief," Selene sighed. "You'll have to forgive her, Sal. Cora wastes all her magical talents making candles."

"Oh, yes. Lavender told me about your shop. It seems very … quaint." He grinned as if at a private joke. "Obin Amorath was a famed alchemist who came to prominence while trotting around the globe in the 1920s. He was as brilliant an explorer as he was a spellworker, and a true lover of puzzles."

"You make him sound like Indiana Jones."

"I suppose it's an apt comparison. Amorath never had children, but he wanted to leave a legacy behind. An immortality project, if you will. Since his specialty lay in creating magical artifacts, he took one last trip around the world and scattered various treasures from his estate everywhere he went. The Tome is the key to finding them"

"So the *Odyssey of Obin Amorath* is like a giant treasure map?"

"A collection of treasure maps, yes. Most of them have been puzzled out by now, of course. But some of the mysteries still remain unsolved, which makes it a highly valuable book indeed." Sal's eyes glittered.

"How did you get this fancy book in the first place, then?" Selene asked with a dubious glance. "I wouldn't think anyone would want to sell it."

"It was a gift from one of my dearly departed colleagues on the Arcane Council. I was most surprised, as was everyone else on the council as this particular volume had been believed missing for some time."

"How much is a book like that worth?" I asked.

"Well, I would never dream of selling it, you understand," he said, clearing his throat and casting his gaze downward. "I consider possession of this tome to be a great responsibility. But out of idle curiosity, I put some feelers out on the open market. Suffice it to say, one could buy a home such as my own many times over from the sale of one such book."

"Aunt Lavender's never cared about money, though." I shook my head. "Are you sure she's the one who took it from you?"

Sal's expression turned steely. "Of course I am. I don't go waving those types of books around for just anyone. I trusted Lavender." He paused and shook his head once, and I wondered if he was more frustrated with himself or with my aunt. "I showed it to Lavender, thinking it might help her in the hunt for the death mask. Then I was called away to tend to some important business. When I returned, Lavender was in the middle of her work and no longer in the mood for conversation, so I left her alone. Only after she left that evening did I notice the book was gone. And ever since then, I've been trying to reach her, to get it back."

Selene and I exchanged a look. "Right. Well, look, Mr. Greco—I mean, Sal. We'll keep our eye out for that book, all right? If I find it while I'm cleaning up my aunt's house, I'll be sure to return it to you."

A smile creased his face. "That is a most generous

offer. I'll be more than willing to reward you for such a service."

"No need. If my aunt borrowed the book, I feel it's my responsibility to return it to you."

The conversation quickly wrapped up when it became apparent that Salvatore didn't have any idea who would want to kidnap Lavender. He insisted that he hadn't told anyone else about his suspicion that she'd swiped the *Odyssey of Obin Amorath*, but as he escorted us back to the front door, I wondered if he was telling the truth.

He saw us outside and with good grace wished us luck in our quest to find Lavender before waving goodbye.

"Do you think someone else found out that Lavender had the book?" I asked Selene once we were in the car. "It would be quite the motive to kidnapping her, if it's really as valuable as he claims."

Selene frowned. "I don't know. I need brain food if we're going to try and do any more theorizing tonight."

"All right, we can think about dinner—"

"Call Clint back and tell him we want sushi."

"I hate sushi."

"I know," Selene said, her teeth flashing. "That way there will be plenty of leftovers."

4

*S*leep was nearly impossible to find that night. My thoughts kept revolving like a motorized merry-go-round that cranked up the speed every few minutes. I lay in bed, staring at the ceiling, trying to figure out my next move. If someone had taken Aunt Lavender because of Salvatore's book, we'd need to figure out who knew she had it. But Sal hadn't been any help, insisting he hadn't told anyone. Lavender might have mentioned it to someone, and as with most small towns, Winterspell had an active grapevine. Though I wasn't sure who would be salivating over rare book gossip. Generally, the things that circulated the fastest were what I liked to call soap opera stories: who was having an affair, whose kid got busted for smoking under the bleachers, who was visiting the local healers for a little cosmetic magic procedure.

In a way, that was helpful. There was a smaller handful of people who would care about a valuable book. The problem was, I had no idea who those people were. Sure, I went to a book club once a month, but that was more about the chef-prepared snacks, fine wine, and good gossip than the books themselves. Not to mention the books we read (or pretended to read) weren't musty alchemical tomes.

I supposed I could go to the library and ask around. Maybe there was a more highbrow book club in town that I didn't know about. Francine, the head librarian, was plugged in to the erudite circles both inside and outside of Winterspell. She might have an idea.

Of course, it all might be a wild goose chase. The book was the closest thing to a motive we'd uncov-ered so far, but even still, it seemed fairly weak. If someone found out Lavender had the book, why kidnap her? Why not break in and steal the book when she was gone? Granted, Selene and I had been looking through Lavender's house for the better part of the last two weeks and we hadn't come across it. Had her assailant tried finding it on their own, and then escalated to kidnapping when they came up empty-handed? Were they keeping her captive until she revealed its location? And if so, why wouldn't she just tell them? What could possibly be in the book that was worth risking her safety or even her life for?

Dark thoughts rolled through my mind until I mustered up the strength to banish them. My brain still wasn't tired enough to sleep though, so instead, it decided to bring up my more personal worries. As Selene had suggested-slash-ordered, I'd called Clint back after leaving Salvatore's house and offered to meet for an early dinner. As I'd expected, he'd had a rough day with his mother and needed an escape. He talked about her over the course of the meal, and while I'd done my best to sympathize, I had a hard time focusing. I think he must have been able to tell, because he excused himself not too long after the bill was paid and didn't press to come to my place for a movie or nightcap.

Round and round and round my thoughts spun, until I finally gave up, tossed aside the covers, and got out of bed. It was nearing four o'clock in the morning. The sun would be rising in a couple of hours. My shop, Wicked Wicks, wasn't set to open for nearly four. This gave me a big enough window to go out and try to clear my mind, and there was only one place that might help.

I dressed quickly, then tiptoed out of the house, careful not to disturb Selene. My house wasn't a shack, as she'd called it, but it was small and at present, the cat slept in a basket out in the living room, which made it hard for me to do much of anything without her noticing. I wanted a cup of coffee, but didn't want to risk waking her up with the grinder and other jostling sounds that it would require. Out in my garage, I loaded my kayak onto the roof of my car and set out toward the lake.

It was a short drive, one of the major selling points when I'd purchased the home a few years ago. Well, when my ex-husband, Roger, and I had purchased it, that is. He was an avid kayaker as well. It was actually how we'd first met, out on the water. Of course, now that we'd been divorced for over a year and a half, that all seemed like it had happened in something of another life.

Banishing those memories, I quickly parked the car in the empty lot and lugged my kayak down to the water. After putting on a life vest, I pulled a knit hat over my unstyled pixie-cut hair to fight off the morning chill. There was no doubt the seasons were changing. With an exhale, I slipped my legs into the hull and shoved off with my paddle. The vessel glided over the gently lapping waters of the lake as I settled into a rhythmic paddling. Sometimes it reminded me of a dance, the way the movements felt, with nature's song propelling me along. Although this morning, even the earliest of early birds didn't seem to be awake. I reached the dead center of the lake and closed my eyes, enjoying the peaceful, still silence. All I could hear was the gentle slap of water against the hull of the kayak, the breeze moving through the surrounding trees, and my own heartbeat.

Right then and there, my problems seemed so far away, both figuratively and literally. I floated there for a while, and then made a circuit of the lake as the sky began to brighten. The birds stirred awake and began to chirp and trill, greeting the coming sun. I continued paddling, not in a hurry to get to any particular place, and lost track of time, just enjoying the simple pleasure of being on the water.

Eventually, my stomach began rumbling, and my need for a caffeine infusion won out, so I paddled back to shore. A few other early morning enthusiasts were arriving at the small parking lot and I waved to a few on my way back to my vehicle. I loaded the boat back on my car and took off my life vest. Then I extracted my phone and checked the time. Six-thirty. Still plenty of time before I needed to be at the shop. I decided to text Leanna. She may not be a water person, but she is most definitely a coffee person.

I knew she would be awake already, probably having just finished her morning yoga flow. So, we played text-me, text-you for a few minutes hammering out the details, and decided to meet at Dragon's Gold Coffee Co., Winterspell's most popular coffee house.

We met outside the coffee house a few minutes later. Leanna parked her Toyota Camry and hurried to meet me by the shop's front door. Leanna's smile is the type that lights up a room. She's bubbly, effer-vescent, and her energy is too much for some people to take. I believe we balance each other out well. I find her exuberance refreshing, and she finds my more practical nature grounding.

"Hey, you." She beamed a smile and came to embrace me on the sidewalk. She smelled of lavender and sunshine. "You're up early."

"Couldn't sleep," I said with a slight smile and a shrug as we parted.

Leanna quirked a perfectly manicured brow at me. "Everything all right? Any news about your aunt?"

"Not yet." I shook my head. I'd filled her in on most of the story, from Selene's arrival to the strange vision the cat had after her fur got mixed in with a powerful memories candle. She also knew I'd been spinning my wheels trying to get the Winter-spell PD involved. Beyond that, there wasn't much to say.

I tugged open the glass door and waited for Leanna to go inside first. We took our place in line, behind three other people who all looked like they could fill in as extras on the set of *The Walking Dead* as they waited to order their coffee.

"I need a distraction," I told Leanna, "tell me what's going on with you. Didn't you go on a date last night?"

Leanna blew out a sigh. "Oh, just wait until I tell you about this guy. You are not going to believe it."

"Oh boy," I said, though I couldn't help but smile a little. Leanna's adventures in online dating were always entertaining. "What's the deal with the new guy?"

"His name is Tyrone, and he's sweet, funny, cute ..."

"Okay …? What's the catch? Does he have an overbearing mother or something?"

"Oh no, he lives on his own. It's not that at all."

"Then what is it?"

"I can't even believe I have to say this, but …" she rolled her eyes to the ceiling. "He's an Elvis invoker."

"Like, he dresses up as Elvis or something?" I laughed. "Does he at least look good in the outfit? Takes a certain kind of man to pull off all those tassels."

"Oh, no no," Leanna said, putting her hand on my bicep. "He's not an Elvis impersonator. He's an Elvis *invoker*. He summons the ghost of the King to perform at birthday parties and such."

"Oh." I blinked. "That's … different."

"Yeah, so he's constantly making peanut butter bacon and banana sandwiches, and you know the smell of roasting bananas makes me nauseous."

I pressed my lips together to keep from breaking out in a giggle fit as we shuffled forward a few paces.

"I don't even think it's the real Elvis," Leanna continued, her expression pained. "I think it might be the spirit of an actual Elvis impersonator, but when I asked Tyrone about it he got all kinds of offended. I honestly thought he was going to ask me to leave."

Still stifling a grin, I gave her my best sympathetic look. "So, what are you going to do?"

Leanna shrugged her slender shoulders. "Either break up with him or start wearing nose plugs, I guess."

Her eyes sparkled as she continued. "Just count yourself lucky you found a man with a real job. How are things going with that most eligible bachelor, anyway?"

"Well … things are going okay, but …"

"Uh-oh, there's a *but?*"

I sighed. "I'm worried that if I get attached, he's just going to leave me when his mother … doesn't need him any longer." I sighed. "Terrible, right? He's dealing with an ailing parent and all I can think of is how it's going to affect me."

"Someone who's been burned once has earned the right to be cautious." We moved forward to our place as the next in line at the counter, then Leanna fixed me with a frank stare. "It sounds to me like you and Clint need to have … 'the talk.'"

"What talk?"

"DTR, babe. Define the relationship. You need to sit down and figure out where you both stand, and what you both want out of the relationship."

"I don't know. I feel like we might need a 'talk' to talk about whether we should have *that* talk," I said with a laugh.

Leanna grinned. "I hear you. Although it's worth remembering that he doesn't have to be your Mr. Right. He could be just your Mr. Right Now. There's nothing wrong with that. Not every relationship has to turn into something long term."

"That's what you said about Greyson, and I'm pretty sure you only kept him around because he was a total neat freak and you wanted to wait to dump him until after he finished reorganizing your pantry."

"Uh, number one, I only dated him for like half a month, and two, my baseboards have never been cleaner."

We shared a laugh and then stepped to the counter to place our order with the barista working the register. I insisted on paying, since it had been my idea to meet up, but Leanna slipped a little extra into the tip jar before we moved to the other end of the counter to wait for our drinks.

AFTER COFFEE, Leanna and I parted ways. She had to get to work, and I needed to get the shop open for the day. Although as she was getting into her car, I made her promise to text me a video of the Elvis invoker's routine. If for no other reason than Selene would probably get a big kick out of it.

As I pulled into a parking spot a few spaces down from my shop, my phone rang. It was Clint. My stomach squirmed as I reached for the phone to answer his call. Was he about to tell me he'd decided he wasn't in a place to get involved with anyone? Maybe we were skipping "the talk" and moving straight to the break-up. He had been acting awfully weird the night before.

I finally answered, just before the call got kicked to voicemail. "Hello?"

"Hey, Cora," Clint said. "It's just me. Is this a bad time?"

"Um, no, not really," I said, trying not to let my trepidation show in my voice. "What's up?"

"Well, I'm actually standing on your front porch, with coffee and pastries, being stared down by a very angry looking cat."

"Where's my breakfast, you bum?" Selene hollered across the line.

"Oh crap," I said with a sigh. "I forgot to fill her bowl before I left."

"Now it better be served to me in bed," Selene snapped.

"I'm sorry about her. I went out for an early morning kayak ride, and then Leanna and I just went out for coffee …"

"No problem. I should have figured you were busy."

I cringed. "No, no. It's okay. Listen, I'll be there in just a few minutes."

"No rush, I've got Selene to keep me company," he said with a soft chuckle.

"That's what I'm worried about. I'm on my way."

I ended the call and blew out an exasperated sigh as I flipped my car into reverse and backed out of the parking spot. I still had a little time before I needed to be at the shop, but my belly was filled with anxiety as I drove home. That, though, was more likely due to the fact that I didn't know what Selene might be saying to Clint in my absence. She was short-tempered and cantankerous in the best of times, so when she got hangry … well, look out world. She might blurt something out to Clint just to spite me, as some kind of payback for forgetting to fill her bowl before I left for the lake.

Leanna's advice ricocheted through my mind one final time as I pulled into my driveway behind Clint's black BMW. As I climbed out of the car, Clint rose from one of the painted Adirondack chairs on my small front porch. He had a drink carrier in his hands holding a pair of coffee cups, and a brown paper bag was sitting on the small bamboo table nestled between the two chairs.

He flashed a smile my way, which I returned as I trod up the steps. Even when he was dressed down, he still pulled off an elegant grace. He wasn't the type to wear ratty t-shirts from his college days, or jeans with faded patches or tears at the corners of the pockets. Everything about Clint, from his precise haircut to his choice of footwear, spoke to his wealth. I wasn't sure just how much money he had, but he'd been raised in a wealthy family, and now ran a successful consulting business in Chicago.

I wasn't able to admire the handsome man for long, as a glowering cat stole my attention while glaring at me from her perch on the flat-topped newel of the porch railing. "It's about time," Selene groused. "You could have at least left a note."

"I thought you would come and find me at the shop when you got hungry. You know I keep extra food there for the days you sleep in late," I replied, doing my best not to snap at the fussy cat. We both knew that she would have been equally annoyed if I'd woken her up at four in the morning when I left the house, and even if I'd thought ahead and filled her bowl, then she would have complained that her food had been sitting out too long and accused me of trying to give her food poisoning.

Ignoring her glower, I stepped over to Clint. "This is a nice surprise," I told him with a smile.

He shuffled the coffee carrier to one hand and used the other to pull me in for a hug. "I'm glad to hear you say that. I wanted to apologize for the way I kind of bolted on you last night."

Frowning, I pulled away and peered up at him. I was a card-carrying member of the short girls club, whereas Clint stood at about six feet tall and had several inches on me. "What do you mean?"

"I wasn't feeling like myself, and I—"

"Can we put a pin in this after-school special till I've had my breakfast?" Selene interrupted.

Sighing, I turned away from Clint and went to open the front door. Selene raced ahead, making a beeline for the kitchen. "I'm sorry about her," I said to Clint as we followed her inside.

Clint was a good sport and waited patiently while I attended to my feline lord and master. "You don't need to apologize," he said. "I know it's just Selene being Selene."

Selene poked her head up from her bowl and gave him an appraising stare, as though she couldn't figure out whether to take umbrage or not.

I smiled wryly at the cat and then turned back to Clint. "Anyway, as you were saying, about last night …" I prompted.

"Oh, right." Clint's soft brown gaze widened. "Well, I mostly wanted to tell you that I know I haven't been the best of companions the past few days. I don't want you to think I'm always this tense and edgy." He smiled softly. "I really can be fun from time to time, believe it or not."

I returned his smile. "I know that. And I also understand what you're going through. You're allowed to have off days. I'm a pretty tough chick, I can handle some mood swings from time to time."

Clint set the coffee and bag of pastries on my dining table, then reached for me. "Come here," he said, his voice turning sultry. My stomach swooped as he pulled me into his arms, and the doubts and question marks that had plagued me were suddenly gone. He kissed me passionately, and my thoughts ceased altogether.

Well, until Selene started hacking up a hairball right behind us.

I SPENT the remainder of the day floating in a happy bubble as I went about my normal routine. Clint stayed at my house long enough to enjoy the coffees and pastries together, then he went to set up camp at the library, one of the places in town that had a decent WiFi signal and a quiet environment for him to get some work done. After he left, I headed back to Wicked Wicks to open for the day.

Selene tried to get on my nerves throughout the day, but I was in such a good mood that it all sort of rolled off me. Clint was coming back over after I got done with work, and I had a feeling it was going to be a very romantic evening. Granted, I might have to lock Selene in a closet in order to fully enjoy myself.

The day passed quickly. Things had slowed down considerably from the peak of the summer tourist blitz, but I still had a steady stream of regulars and a slew of custom candle orders that kept me plenty busy. Additionally, I'd switched over to my off-season hours, and was able to close up two hours earlier than I did in the summertime. Even still, I closed up a few minutes before six, eager to get to where the night was heading, and hurried back to my house to change and freshen up before Clint's arrival.

"Should I go with the red or the black?" I asked Selene, gesturing down at my feet, one of which was slipped into a black pump, while the other modeled a red stiletto. Truth be told, I wasn't much of a girly-girl, and had a terrible time when it came to picking out clothes. I also had a figure that was tough to fit. I was short and curvy, and while I didn't mind the extra padding, it did sometimes make it hard to find outfits that flattered my shorter torso and larger chest without then skewing the other way and making my legs look shorter and thicker.

Clint had seen me in the red dress once before, when he'd inadvertently stumbled into a busy Ladies Night at the local tavern. He'd been distraught, but even still, I remembered the spark in his eyes when he spotted me in the crowded bar.

Selene, on the other hand, was not interested in

playing fashion show. "Who do I look like, Heidi Klum?"

I rolled my eyes as I turned around to face my full-length mirror. I lifted one foot, tottered a little, and quickly put it back down before I wound up breaking an ankle.

"Now what are you doing? Some kind of flamingo impression?" the cat asked.

"Black it is," I said with an exhale. "I'm pretty sure there's a rule about wearing red shoes with a red dress anyway. Leanna would know for sure."

"I don't know why you're bothering to go through all of this trouble," Selene said. "This is yet another example of where cats, and the rest of the animal kingdom, I suppose, have it figured out. Mating is much easier when you don't have to go to these lengths."

I cringed. "Can we maybe not call it *mating*?"

"What would you like to call it? Knocking boots? Getting frisky? Doing the no-pants dance?"

"Selene, enough!" I huffed a frustrated grunt as I switched out the red stiletto for the matching black pump. "You know, this is exactly why I want you to make yourself scarce tonight."

The cat reared back. "Excuse me?"

"You heard me," I growled. "I think it would be

best if you weren't home when Clint and I get back from dinner."

"I see how it is." Selene jumped down from the foot of the bed and stalked out of the room, her tail held high.

Great. I could already imagine the ways she was plotting to get her revenge.

*a*s it turned out, all of my agonizing over shoes was a little bit in vain. Clint arrived on my doorstep promptly at six-thirty, as we'd agreed, but instead of being dressed in his usual suit and tie, or even stiffly pressed dark-wash jeans and button-up shirt, he looked like he'd walked into an REI, pointed at a mannequin, and ordered one of everything it was wearing. He wore cargo pants, a waffle thermal, a puffer jacket with reflective strips on the sleeves and back, and a pair of hiking boots. Very expensive hiking boots.

We stared at each other, both taken a little aback, and then we both burst out laughing.

"I can go change—" we both said at the same

time, each gesturing over our respective shoulders, before laughing all over again.

"Oy, and you thought you had to force me to leave," Selene grumbled as she trotted out the front door. "Get me out of here before you start singing 'Opposites Attract' or something."

Clint chuckled. "I guess that would make me the cartoon wolf in this scenario. Because in that dress, you're definitely giving '80s-era Paula Abdul a run for her money."

My cheeks warmed. "Thank you."

"I wanted to surprise you with a sunset hike around the lake," Clint added after a moment. "I know you like to spend time outdoors, and while I might be a city slicker now, I used to run through these trails when I was here with my family in the summertime."

"Really?" I asked, my eyes wide. "I somehow have a hard time picturing that."

Clint laughed. "I know. I know. But I've been thinking it's time to get back to my roots a little. It feels right." He gave me a meaningful look, his expression turning more serious. "I really like spending time with you, Cora. I want to do whatever makes you happy."

His eyes practically smoldered, and it was all I

could do not to turn to jelly. "I like spending time with you, too, Clint."

He reached for me, letting his fingertips drift softly over my cheek before he tipped my face upward and brought his lips to mine. My heart beat so hard in my chest, I thought for sure he must be able to feel it against his own.

We parted all too soon, breathless and wild. "I suppose we could save the hike for another time," Clint suggested with a half-cocked smile. "But we do have to put these boots to use sooner or later, because I spent a small fortune on them."

I laughed and grabbed for the front of his shirt, playfully dragging him inside.

LATER THAT NIGHT, when Clint and I got around to ordering some delivery from Elephant's Palace, I brought him up to speed on everything that had happened the day before and explained why I hadn't been answering some of his recent calls.

Clint listened patiently. It was one of my favorite things about him, I decided. He was a good listener and saved his questions until I was done speaking. "Is there a chance this Sal guy is the one who kidnapped your aunt?" he asked. "Maybe he's been leaving the messages on her answering machine to kind of provide an alibi for himself. The cops wouldn't think he had anything to do with it if he's been calling her, acting like he doesn't know a thing about her abduction."

I canted my head to the side. "I don't know. He's pretty old. Selene says that in her vision, she saw the assailant, but they were dressed all in black and wore a mask, and from their body type alone, she couldn't determine whether they were male or female. But to carry Aunt Lavender over their shoulder … I don't know. My aunt is petite, like me, but us Hearth women tend to carry a little extra, um, padding."

Clint leveled me with a sly grin. "And thank the goddess for that."

My cheeks warmed as I smiled and ducked my chin, pretending to study the piece of garlic naan on the edge of my plate.

"In any case," I continued, "I don't think Salvatore would have been strong enough to haul her out like that. But, I guess it's possible he could have hired someone to take her. Maybe he wanted to intimidate her into telling him where the book is."

"And you haven't found it in the house?" Clint asked, then stopped himself and laughed. "Not that I'd be surprised. That place was really something."

I sighed. "Tell me about it. Selene and I have gone over there almost every day for the past two weeks and it's *still* barely contained chaos. If the book is there, it's either hiding in plain sight amongst the wreckage or it's locked away in some secret cubby that only Lavender knows about."

"How come Selene doesn't know anything about it?" Clint asked as he used his own naan to scoop up a generous amount of tikka masala. "You said she used to be your aunt's familiar before she came to live with you."

"She was. But I guess my aunt was kind of blocking Selene out. Keeping doors closed, not bothering to try and loop her into whatever she was researching. Honestly, Selene is a little bitter about it. Not that she'd ever admit it in so many words, but she gets defensive and upset if I try to poke too much into the workings of their relationship."

"Hmm." Clint took a bite.

"The past couple of months haven't been easy for her," I added. "I try to remind myself that her feelings have been hurt, but she makes it so hard for me to be too sympathetic."

Clint nodded thoughtfully. "I get that. It's the same thing with my mother." He paused and held up a hand. "Not that I want to talk about her tonight, but I want you to know I understand how you feel. It's hard trying to help someone work through things when they're actively trying to repel you. Or at least, it seems like they are."

I smiled and placed my hand over his on the table. "It is. But you're doing a good job. Especially after the way she treated you in the aftermath of Seth's death. I can't imagine too many people would have volunteered to stick around after all of that. You're a good man, Clint. And a good son, no matter what she might say."

Clint paused, his eyes glossing over before he quickly blinked a few times. "Thank you, Cora. That really does mean a lot to me. For what it's worth, I think you're doing a good job with Selene, too. I honestly don't know how you do it. I think I'd have been tempted to drop her off at the Humane Society or something."

I smiled. "Yeah, I guess I'm just a big marshmallow or something."

He chuckled and traced his fingers along my jaw. "You have a good heart."

A soft thump sounded in the kitchen, and

Selene's voice called out, "You two done making the beast with two backs, yet?"

Clint choked on his water.

My cheeks went red hot. "Oh. My. Goddess."

With some trouble, Clint managed to swallow just as the cat came stalking into the living room, her tail held high overhead. "Oh, good. You're both dressed. Listen, I've been thinking, and I've decided we need to go and ask Sal some more questions about that book. The man didn't even give us a basic description of the thing. How does he expect us to find it in that disaster of a library Lavender keeps? And on top of that, if he thinks she stole it why did he wait until now to start calling her about it? I was just over at Lavender's place and I checked the answering machine. The only message was the one we heard yesterday."

"Really?" I blinked. "But didn't he say he'd been trying to get ahold of her for weeks now?"

"Mhmm." Selene twitched her whiskers. "I smell a rat."

I glanced at the clock on the living room wall. "It's too late to call or swing by there tonight. It will have to wait until tomorrow." I met Selene's gaze and then slid my eyes to the right, hoping she'd pick up on the signal and take her leave once more.

Instead, the cat narrowed her blue eyes at me. "You need *more* time?" She shifted her stare to Clint and raised her chin. "Hmm. I may have underestimated you."

"Sweet baby beluga whale," I muttered, burying my face in my hands. "I must have been a serial killer in a past life to deserve this kind of karma."

SELENE KEPT her peace until the morning, but as soon as Clint and I poked our heads out from my bedroom, she was on us like white on rice. "Finally!" she exclaimed, swirling once around my ankles as I tried to make my way to the kitchen.

"Hey! Need I remind you that if you trip me and I break my back, we won't be going anywhere for a solid year?" I groused as I kicked at the air where she just was a moment before. "We're having coffee and breakfast first, Selene. I'm not going to show up on Salvatore's doorstep at seven o'clock in the morning."

Clint smiled at me. "Want me to run out and get provisions?"

"No need. I have plenty of coffee and there are some eggs in the fridge I need to use up."

"Whew. Now if that's not romance, I don't know what is," Selene quipped. "Hey, honey, how do you feel about nearly rotten eggs?"

I rolled my eyes and ignored her. "I got them at the farmer's market last weekend," I told Clint.

"I wasn't too worried," he replied.

Selene hovered like a relentless mosquito as Clint and I enjoyed a simple meal of eggs and toast, with a pot of coffee on the side. Clint seemed to be capable of drinking almost as much coffee as me in the morning. If he was going to stay over on a more regular basis, I'd need to start buying a full pound per week at the market.

There was something strange and yet comfortable about the slow-paced morning with Clint. It was the first time I'd had a man stay over since … well, since Roger. Sure, I'd dated a little here and there since the divorce, but never got anywhere close to this kind of experience. It was nice, though, sharing the start of the day with someone. Especially someone as handsome as Clint.

When we finished, he jumped up to rinse the dishes and load them in my compact dishwasher before finishing the dregs from his mug. "You have excellent taste in coffee," he told me. "What blend is this?"

"Single origin, actually. Costa Rican."

"And she dares to complain about *my* expensive tastes," Selene interjected from her perch at the other end of the counter. Before I could argue with her, she jumped down. "Are we ready to go now?"

"Tell you what, why don't you go wait by the car. We'll be there in five," I told her.

She gave me a skeptical look, but then slipped through the cat flap she'd forced me to install in the back door.

"You don't have to come along," I told Clint once she was gone. "I'm sure you've got work stuff to do, and once we're done at Sal's, I need to get to the shop."

Clint hitched one shoulder. "I don't mind tagging along." Smiling, he reached for me and wrapped his arms around my waist. "But either way, are you free for dinner tonight?"

"Hmm." I tapped a finger against my lips and grinned. "I suppose."

"Good answer." He kissed me quickly before he let me go. "Then we can annoy Selene with classic 'I don't know, where do you want to go?' conversations all the way to Sal's house."

With a wicked grin, I started down the hall to get changed out of my pajamas. "I like the way you think."

We rode in Clint's BMW to Salvatore's estate. Selene insisted on riding in the front seat, so I went along with Clint's plan to be as annoying as possible. Which was working, until Selene threatened to dig her claws into the heated leather seats. That shut Clint and me up in a hurry.

I gave Clint the final two directions and we pulled into the driveway. It almost surprised me that the home didn't have a gated entrance, but then, for all I knew there were magical wards protecting the property if no one was home. A lot of Winterspell homes utilized magical security systems, just in case.

"It looks like he's home," I said, gesturing at the front of the house. The windows were open and as we stepped out of Clint's car, we could hear soft piano music playing from somewhere inside.

Clint took my hand as we stepped onto the porch, the music growing louder, some kind of piano concert. I rapped on the door and waited. Nothing happened.

"Mr. Greco?" I knocked again, harder.

"Hmm. Maybe he's not home after all," I said, starting to turn away.

"Or he can't hear us over that dreadful music!" Selene retorted. A *crack* of magic slammed into the door as Selene sent a puff of pink sparks from the tip of her tail.

"Selene!" I hissed.

"What?" She looked up at me. "Just making sure he can hear us."

While I inspected the front door for signs of damage, Clint sidestepped to the large window nearest the door, and peered inside.

"Um, Cora—" The color drained from his face, and he stiffened up.

"What?" I joined him at the window and my heart skipped a beat.

At the foot of the elegant marble staircase lay Salvatore Greco's lifeless body.

6

*I*n a panic, I lunged at the front door and found it unlocked. I shoved it open, and Selene barged inside. She rushed over to Sal's fallen form and placed a paw on his neck, her tail twitching like a metronome. I already knew she wasn't going to find a pulse. There was too much blood, and Sal's chest wasn't rising and falling.

"He's gone," the cat confirmed, before stepping backward, mindful not to get her paws in the blood. "Been that way for a while, I'd say. He's stiffer than one of Gerry's Old-Fashioneds."

Cringing at her choice of words, I gestured for her. "Selene, get back out here. You're contaminating the scene!"

She looked back at me in annoyance. "I'm not contaminating anything."

"You're kidding, right? Do you have any concept of how much you shed? I swear, I've banished every light-colored piece of clothing to the back of my closet."

Clint still looked stunned, but he managed to pull his unblinking stare from Sal's body for a moment. "Um, Cora's probably right, Selene. You should get out of there before the police arrive."

Speaking of which … I reached into my pocket for my cell phone.

"Fine, but I still don't see how a little cat hair could cause a problem. It's not like anyone could think I had something to do with this." Selene padded out onto the porch. "From the looks of things, Sal fell down the stairs and cracked open his brainy little noggin. Are we sure he doesn't have a cat? Because on second thought, that does seem like something one of my kind might have had a paw in."

"We don't know what happened," I told her. "And until we do, it's best to leave the scene undisturbed."

"Okay, Columbo, yeesh."

I called the Winterspell PD and before I could say more than my first and last name, I was transferred through to Sheriff Templeton himself.

"Listen, Sheriff—"

"Oh, for crying out loud, Cora." He heaved a sigh. "I told you we were putting together some plans. You need to give me more than a day or two to sort things out."

"Actually, Sheriff, I'm not calling—"

"Although, I'm still not convinced there's anything to be found. I know that you miss her, and I'm sure that the senile old cat thinks she saw something sinister going on, but I've known Lavender longer than you've been alive. Trust me. One of these days you're going to go by her house, and there will be a trail of smoke going skyward, and she'll be home. Safe and sound, with a whole bunch of malarkey stories to keep the whole town entertained for a while."

"Sheriff—"

"Don't get me wrong. I like hearing those stories as much as the next guy. But the fact of the matter is—"

"Oh, for the goddess's sake, Sheriff Templeton, shut up for a minute and listen to me!" I paused and slapped a hand over my mouth. Clint and Selene both stared at me, slack jawed. Then Selene started to snicker. "I'm so sorry, sir, but please, I'm at Salvatore Greco's house and he's dead!"

There was a long pause, but I wasn't sure what had startled the sheriff more: my admonishment or the news about Salvatore.

Finally, he cleared his throat. "Salvatore Greco's you said?"

"Yes."

A series of shuffling noises and some muffled instructions were barked in the background before the sheriff returned his attention to my call. "I'll be there shortly. Don't leave, and don't touch anything!"

"Right, I—"

The line went dead.

Frowning, I shoved my phone back into my pocket. "Some people have never worked a day in customer service, and it shows," I muttered. "He hung up on me."

Selene was still giving me a starry-eyed look. "When he gets here, do you think you could tell him to *shut up* again? I'd kill to see the look on his face in person."

I rolled my eyes. "That was a mistake. I shouldn't have screamed at him like that."

Selene swished her tail. "Oh, he's had that coming for a while as far as I'm concerned."

"He just wouldn't stop talking about Lavender. He still somehow thinks she's just going to materialize one day." I shook my head and tamped down a fresh wave of anger as I replayed the brief snippet of a conversation in my head. "I swear, he needs to retire already. This town needs new blood in charge of the PD."

"Amen," Selene agreed.

I glanced back inside Salvatore's home, and while I tried to avoid looking at Salvatore himself, my gaze kept gravitating back toward the man. He was bundled into a dressing gown. One foot wore a shearling slipper, while its mate lay halfway down the stairs, suggesting it had come off during the tumble. Selene was probably right. He must have missed a step and fallen to his death. A tragedy, but an accident.

Then, as I circled my gaze through the scene once more, something needled me. "Do you think it's weird that the door was unlocked?"

Clint considered the question for a moment. "Maybe he came out to get the morning paper and forgot to lock up after himself?"

I glanced over my shoulder. "No, the paper is still in the driveway."

"I told you two he's stiff as a drink," Selene interjected, her tone exasperated. "He's been dead for a while now. A good eight hours, if I had to guess."

"Okay, so he forgot to lock up last night," Clint countered with a slight shrug. "Maybe that's what he was coming downstairs to do. He got ready for bed, remembered he hadn't locked up, and then … well, that happened."

"You're probably right. I don't know why I'm overthinking it." I hugged myself and shuddered, even though the day was hardly cold. "It's not like he would be the first aging person to suffer a fall in their own home."

"No, but it does seem like such an ignoble end for such a great adventurer," Selene said. "He used to talk about his trips with Lavender. Imagine climbing both peaks of Kilimanjaro and then meeting your end at the bottom of your own staircase."

"Isn't there only one peak of Kilimanjaro?" Clint asked.

"The second peak is invisible to the mundane. You have to squint out of the corner of your eye and chant a bunch of spells in order to see it."

Clint frowned.

"Selene, don't confuse him." I shook my head. "Or me, for that matter."

"Fine. I'll take myself elsewhere," Selene sniffed, before strutting back into Salvatore's foyer. "I'm going hunting for clues."

"Selene, get back here!" I hissed through clenched teeth. "We're not supposed to go in there. We're supposed to wait for the police!"

"Yeah, I heard Templeton tell you hairless apes to do that. The thing is, he doesn't know the answer to the oldest riddle of time: Why do cats have no lord?"

Selene slinked past Salvatore, then up the stairs, and vanished from sight. I scrubbed a hand down my face. "Good grief. That cat is more trouble than she's worth."

"I heard that!" Selene's voice echoed down to us.

Clint slid a sidelong glance at me. "I wonder if you should start traveling with dehydrated anchovies in your pockets or something. From what I've seen, bribery is the only thing that works on her."

I scrunched up my nose. "Oh, yes. Just what I want. A pocket full of dead fish at all times. Now, that's attractive."

Clint chuckled. "I'd still take you out on a Friday night, fish pockets and all."

I smiled and leaned into him, avoiding looking inside the house. "That's good to know, but I think I'll still pass on the idea. If Selene winds up getting herself thrown in the pokey, that just means I'll get a night or two of peace and quiet before I have to go bail her out."

"Hey, come up here!" Selene called.

"What? Why? Are you in trouble?"

"No, I'm not in trouble. You've just got to see this."

"I can't come in there, Selene. The police said to wait right here and that's what I'm going to do."

"Oh, come on! Don't be such a Goody Two-shoes."

"Am I seriously being peer-pressured by a cat?" I muttered to Clint, before calling back to the feline in question, "Can't you just tell me what you see?"

"Fine," Selene snapped. "But just for the record, you're absolutely no fun. Lavender would have come up here. Heck, she probably would have led the charge!"

"Well, when we find her and bring her back home, you two can go do whatever you want." I paused and winced. "Stars, that's a scary thought."

Selene continued, having not heard my addendum. "There's a half-empty bottle of bourbon on Sal's desk. The seal is sitting in the trash can, so it looks like it was just opened, and there's only one glass. Sal told us he doesn't drink, remember?"

"Well, maybe he was just saying that, Selene," I called up the stairs.

"I don't know about that. In all the times that Lavender and I came here, he never touched booze, even when serving it up to everyone else."

"So, he had a slipup. What are you hinting at?"

I heard Selene land, as if she'd jumped down from a bookcase or desk. "It also looks like someone went through his study," she added. "Stuff is moved around and out of place, and you know how much of a neat freak Sal is. Or … was, I suppose."

The sheriff's brown and white car appeared at the end of the drive. "Selene! Get back down here," I hissed. "Sheriff Templeton is here."

To my utter shock, the cat listened. She reappeared at the top of the stairs and slunk back down to join Clint and me on the porch while Templeton parked his cruiser. He walked up the driveway with one of his deputies and joined us on the porch.

"The ambulance is on its way," Sheriff Templeton said by way of greeting. He peered into the house at the gruesome scene. "Was this door open when you got here?" he asked.

I shook my head. "No. When we saw Salvatore through the window, I opened it. It was unlocked."

"Hmm." Templeton gestured at his deputy, who

went inside and squatted down beside Salvatore, confirming what we all already knew. "And what brought you out here to Mr. Greco's home at this hour?"

I swallowed. "We think he might have had information regarding my aunt. They were friends, and he was probably one of the last people to see her before she was kidnapped."

"You hear that?" Selene interjected. "*K-I-D-N-A-P-P-E-D.*"

Templeton's bushy mustache twitched but he refrained from saying anything on the matter. Instead, he tugged a small notepad from his pocket and pulled a pen free from the metal rings binding the notebook along the top. He gave the pen a decisive click and began asking a series of questions: What time we arrived? Did we see or hear anything or anyone? When was the last time we saw Sal alive?

Templeton was thorough, but seeing as there wasn't much to tell, the process wrapped up rather quickly. By the time we finished, both an ambulance and another squad car of officers had arrived, and Templeton dismissed us in order to shift his full attention to what was happening inside the house.

"What a disaster," I bemoaned as we trooped back to Clint's car. A pinch bit into the side of my neck and I slapped at it. "Dang bugs! I think I just got a mosquito bite."

Selene swished past me. "Oh, poor Cora. The guy in there took a header down the stairs, but you're worried about a bug bite?"

Scowling, I yanked open the passenger-side door and dropped into the leather seat.

We drove back to my place in relative silence. I needed to get to the shop, but I had no idea how I was going to get my head right for a long day of work. It wasn't just the tragedy of Salvatore's death that was hitting me, it was bigger than that. Salvatore was the only lead Selene and I had come up with after two weeks of searching for clues, and now he was gone. Along with any nugget of information he might have had, leaving me to sink back into the mire of hopeless despair. I would do my best to keep treading my way through it, but I couldn't help but feel I was starting to drown.

7

*T*he next morning, I awoke to the sound of a cat puttering around my kitchen. I was all too familiar with the sound of Selene dislodging the butter dish so she could lick the contents, regardless of how many times I asked her to refrain. However, the sounds that followed bore little resemblance to her usual antics. There was lots of metal banging on metal, a thin sound instead of a hammering, followed by the crinkling of paper and the snap of plastic. I rolled over and tried to return to sleep in spite of this cacophony, but it proved a task worthy of Hercules' Twelve Labors.

After another minute or two, I flung aside the covers and dragged myself out of bed. Bleary eyed, I shuffled into the kitchen to see what all the ruckus was about and came upon Selene, ensconced at the kitchen table with the tattered, clawed, chewed remains of the *Winterspell Gazette*. Bits of newspaper fluttered all about in the wind stirred by the ceiling fan, many of them dark with cat slobber. The blue plastic sheath that had housed the paper and protected it from the elements lay in torn shreds all about the tiled kitchen floor, and a bit of the blue plastic still clung to the cat flap.

Following the trail, it was easy to see what had transpired while I hovered on the cusp betwixt wakefulness and slumber. In her eternal impatience, my so-called familiar had clawed the paper fully in through the cat flap, bit and chewed her way through the plastic sheath, dragged the resulting mess up onto the kitchen counter, and proceeded to tear it up even more while trying to find the sections she wished to peruse.

"You know that I'll bring it in and open it for you once I'm awake," I said on my way to the coffee pot. "Then it wouldn't look like something Edward Scissorhands got ahold of."

Ignoring me, Selene tapped one paw against the paper before her. "Check this out. *Salvatore Greco: His Life, His Legacy.* Pretty snazzy headline, right?"

"Not as snazzy as having an intact newspaper," I

muttered. "I also find it fascinating that in all your claimed centuries of life, you've never bothered learning one simple cleaning spell."

Selene scoffed. "Uh, why do you think you have opposable thumbs, except to clean up our trash? Besides, you're just bitter. What would a headline about you read like? *Cora the Witch. She made candles and terrible choices in men. The end.*"

"I see that you're in rare form this morning," I grumbled.

"Thank you for noticing. Hey, listen to this. Salvatore once negotiated peace between two warring tribes of yuppies in the magical ruins of Los Angeles circa A.D. 4000."

I frowned. "A.D. 4000? What are you even talking about?"

"He traveled through time and prevented the hellish nightmare that *would* have been by changing the past. It's all in his memoir, *Salvatore Greco: A Life Most Lived.*"

"Uh-huh. And *I* traveled through time and rode a T-Rex to brunch with Wilma Flintstone," I said with a roll of my eyes. "Do they shelve that book in the memoir section or with the other sci-fi fantasies?"

As far as I was concerned, the only thing about Salvatore's past that was of interest was his connection to my aunt, and what he may have known about her disappearance. If Selene was right, and he'd only left the one voice message on her machine, it seemed to follow that he was keeping some kind of secret. One that he'd now taken to his grave.

"Seems that I'm not the only one in rare form," Selene replied, giving me a curious look over her shoulder. "What's got your granny panties all in a twist?"

I dumped half a bag of coffee beans into the grinder. "Well, for starters, a certain cat woke me up an hour before my alarm was set to go off, and now I'm too awake to go back to sleep."

Selene groaned and turned her focus back to the paper. "The article says he died in a tragic accident at home. So, I guess that means Templeton and his crew aren't bothering to investigate further. Raise your paw if you're surprised!"

She made a show of glancing around the room, before nodding. "As I suspected."

"Don't tell me you're starting to see invisible friends," I teased, feeling a little bit of the gloom lift ever so slightly.

Selene scowled at me. "All I'm saying is that there is clearly more to the story, and the sheriff didn't even bother to ask me for my statement."

"Yeah, and that's probably for the best," I countered. "You would have had to admit to snooping around upstairs after he told us to stay out of the house."

While the coffee beans whirred through the grinder, I retrieved the broom and dustpan and began sweeping up Selene's mess. When the ear-piercing grinder shut off, I paused and looked at the cat. "I have my bones to pick with Templeton, but I'm sure that if there was evidence of foul play, he would follow up on it."

Selene narrowed her eyes. "I can tell by your tone that you don't really believe what you're spewing out of your cake hole. What about the drink? Huh? Salvatore told us he couldn't drink, even a little, and yet he somehow managed to knock back half a bottle of bourbon. How do you explain that?"

"Well, maybe that's what did him in, just like his doctor said." I shrugged and finished sweeping the bits of shredded paper and plastic film into a pile. "He got drunk, didn't feel good, went to go downstairs, and just … fell."

"And what about the rummaged books and opened desk drawers? I supposed he did that while in a drunken stupor, like some kind of lurching sailor on a storm-tossed deck, knocking everything over?"

The cat pantomimed the drunken dance.

"Not quite," I said wryly as I started filling the dustpan. "I was thinking more like he had a few drinks while he was going through his things, and maybe he didn't put them back in the right spot because he was a little drunk. Or, you know, a *lot* drunk."

"All right then, Miss Smarty Pants, how do you explain away the letter in his desk that said, 'you're making a huge mistake, and sooner or later you're going to pay the price for your ego.' What about that, huh? Let's hear you explain that away."

I paused mid-squat. "What?"

"The letter. You know, the one that said, 'you're making a huge mistake, and someday you're going to pay the price for your ego.' Didn't I just mention it?"

"Why didn't you tell me about the letter earlier? And what were you doing going through Salvatore's things, anyway?"

"Well, if you hadn't been so quick to call the police, we might have had the answers by now, but nooooo. You had to be a Girl Scout about it."

I finished sweeping up the mess and carried the dustpan to the trash can by the back door. "Calling the cops is what you're supposed to do when you come across a body, Selene."

"Yeah, if you're a civilian. We're hard-boiled, hard-nosed, hard-drinking detectives."

"No. We're not. Sure, we helped Clint clear his name, but that hardly qualifies us to investigate crimes." I rubbed a hand down my face and sighed. "Okay, so let's just engage in some supposition here. Suppose that it *was* murder for a moment, and not an accident."

"I'm with you so far."

I put the broom and dustpan away, then returned to the other counter to finish making my coffee. "All right, well if it wasn't an accident, and was in fact a cold-blooded murder, then we'd need a motive. Why would someone want Salvatore Greco dead?"

"Good question. Although a rich guy like that is bound to make some enemies on his climb to the top."

"They say there is no greater measure of success than the enemies you make." I sighed. "Of course, that's probably cold comfort to poor Salvatore."

"Poor Salvatore? Let me tell you something about men like Salvatore Greco. They generally get their power by stepping on everyone else on their way to the top. Like crabs in a bucket."

"That's certainly a dark view of things."

Of course, that was par for the course when it came to Selene.

The cat continued laying out her case. "Salvatore worked his way to the top, sure, but then what did he do? Shift his focus to humanitarian efforts? Build a university or some other kind of educational center? No. Sal leveraged it all to make himself even wealthier."

"Okay, but what about the university students he let into his personal library? He said he wanted to help the next generation."

"Oh, sweet, simple Cora. That's called job security. Most of those starry-eyed nerds will find some cushy job in the future, and some of them will go on to become his best customers."

"Customers?" I frowned.

"For his rare book trade. He sells off rare books and pockets the cash without the Arcane Council's knowledge. Some of the books he's sold should have gone straight to the Arcane Council's restricted library, away from the general public, but if Sal did that, he wouldn't get a penny out of the deal. So, he did a little of both. For every rare book he took to the council for applause and admiration, he sold two on the side."

I frowned and considered this. "So, what about the *Odyssey of Obin Amorath*? Should that go to the Arcane Council?"

"Probably. I haven't seen it for myself, but books like that usually have some kind of dark magic. If Odin's clues and treasure hunts were all aboveboard, the puzzles would have all been solved by now. And even if it doesn't, it should be preserved and put in a museum for everyone to enjoy."

"I had no idea you felt so strongly about the matter," I told her, genuinely surprised by her resolve. Normally, Selene struck me as the kind of person (well, person*ish*) that was only out for herself. So, to hear her rail against someone she perceived as being too selfish was something of a head scratcher.

"Well, I do." She sniffed.

"If you despised the guy so much, why are you sitting here fawning about his memoir and obituary?"

"Who said I despised him?" she asked. "Just because I didn't agree with his business practices doesn't mean I hated his guts. He led an interesting life. I like interesting people. Besides, he could be the link we need to find Lavender."

"I think you mean he could have *been* our link. He's not much use to us now," I muttered darkly.

"Although now that you mention this thing about the book trade, I'm even more convinced he told other people that he suspected Lavender took the book. Remember how he said he wasn't going to sell it—"

"Which was of course a bald-faced lie," Selene interrupted.

"Maybe so, but he did say he'd sent out some feelers, to get a sense of its value," I continued. "What if he was earnest about not selling it? And what if one of those would-be customers got upset that he'd dangled a juicy carrot and then yanked it back?"

Selene's eyes gleamed. "See, now you're thinking like a real detective!"

I poured my mug of coffee. The first one of the day I took straight-up. Creamy lattes were meant for later in the day. My sweet tooth didn't tend to kick in until after lunch.

"Sadly, I won't be of much use today," I told Selene. "I'm behind on custom orders, so I'll be at Wicked Wicks all day."

Saturdays were generally my biggest sales days. Even in the off-season, the residents of Winterspell tend to do their retail therapy on the weekends, which is why I opted to only close the shop entirely on Wednesdays to give myself a day off rather than taking a proper weekend.

"I'll see what I can find out on my own," Selene said, already jumping down from the table.

"Okay, but be good," I called after her as she darted through the cat flap. "Yeah. That's about as likely as a vampire going vegetarian."

I OPENED Wicked Wicks for the day and within a few minutes, I already had a stream of customers. The early risers in town, who wanted to kick off their errands first thing. Not that I minded. They tended to be some of my most loyal regulars. I made small talk with most of them and helped them make decisions on their purchases.

Throughout the morning, more people filtered in. The nice thing about this time of year is that most of my customers are repeat buyers, and they already know what they want. They might have a question or two here and there, but I didn't have to stop and explain the basics to every person who walked through the door. It helped me find that balance between creating and selling, as I minded the shop.

I worked the sales floor, I worked the register, and occasionally I rushed into the back to grab more stock to replenish my shelves. It's hard to complain about being busy. My mother has a saying, 'business is never bad,' meaning don't complain when you're busy at work.

I wasn't one to spend a lot of time complaining—unless it was about Selene—but I will say that by the time I closed up shop around six in the evening, I had barely sat down for more than the ten minutes it took to wolf down a sandwich for lunch, and my feet were feeling it. With the door locked, I eased myself down onto a stool I kept behind the counter and sighed. I eyed the shop with a weary eye as I slipped out of my shoes. The place was a disorganized mess. Candy wrappers and bits of detritus tracked in from other shops littered the floor. There's a trash can right near the shop's front door, but people tended to miss it.

Candles were toppled over, put away in the wrong area, or lying on the floor in some cases. I gave myself a few minutes to rest my aching feet and then got to work on what we in the retail industry refer to as "recovery." It's a fancy way to say picking up after a horde of customers have run roughshod on your establishment and your merchandise. Recovery took a solid twenty minutes, and then I turned my attention to counting the till.

For my efforts, I wound up with a solid six hundred dollars in my cash deposit envelope, and that accounted for only about half the day's sales, as a lot of people preferred to use a credit or debit card for their purchase. Hard on the feet, but good on the wallet. That's another one I learned from my mother.

After filling out my account info on the envelope, I let my eyes close and enjoyed the silence of the shop. It had been buzzing with the hum of customer conversation all day long.

I cracked an eyelid because something didn't feel right. Something was wrong, but what? I couldn't put my finger on it. Then it hit me.

Selene. This was exactly the point in the day when Selene would have been messing with me: when I was trying to relax and was in a vulnerable state. Yet Selene was nowhere to be found.

In fact, I realized that she hadn't been at the shop all day. I usually left the back door cracked open with a rubber door stopper in case she wanted to come and go while I worked. I wasn't sure what we were going to do in another month or so when it became too cold to leave the door propped open like that, but we'd cross that bridge when we got to it. I looked about the shop, checking and double-checking the stock room to be sure she hadn't been trapped in a cardboard box—one of her favorite places to nap—but it was to no avail.

When Selene is around, it's generally bad for me. When she goes AWOL, it's generally bad for the population of Winterspell at large. She was like an irritated Manhattanite, stomping through the streets, just waiting for someone to cut in front of her or almost hit her with their car, so she could have someone to harangue and insult. And while Winterspell was a town full of magical creatures and beings, Selene was—so far as I knew—the only talking animal. So when she starts screaming at someone on the sidewalk, it tends to cause quite a scene.

I locked up the shop and hopped onto my bike. I pedaled around the downtown shopping district, keeping my eyes peeled for the small gray cat. I didn't see her anywhere, and my anxiety only began to grow. After a couple of laps, I gave up searching downtown and instead rode all the way to Aunt Lavender's house.

A quick glance around proved fruitless. No sign of the old cat. Selene is no spring chicken, and despite her story about being invincible, I was almost certain that she wasn't. On top of that, she was also the sole eyewitness to Aunt Lavender's abduction. If something happened to her ...

Eventually, I grew frustrated. I couldn't find Selene anywhere. I wound up riding home, hoping she'd returned from terrorizing the neighborhood, which was quite likely, since it was around the time she usually started caterwauling for her dinner.

As I turned at the intersection onto my street, I spotted a black BMW in my driveway and my heart did a somersault.

I leaned my bike up against the house, not bothering to put it in the garage just yet, and rushed inside to find Selene and Clint, sitting tête-à-tête at my dining room table.

"There you are," I sighed. "I just rode all over town looking for you."

Clint smiled. "I'm assuming you mean Selene."

"Yes. Although I am happy to see you, too. Of course."

Clint stood to come and embrace me. "Since when are you two partners?" I asked with a quirked brow.

"You two can go be lovey-dovey another time," Selene snapped. "I have something much more important to say!"

"Okay …?"

"I know who killed Sal!" Selene said triumphantly. She got up and did a little dance on the table, shaking her tail like it held a maraca. "I'm thinking about running for sheriff in the next election. I'm about to go two for two here!"

"Oh, may the goddess help us all."

8

"*A*re you just going to stand there staring at me? Or are you going to ask me who the killer is?"

I let my purse drop from my shoulder and set it on the nearest kitchen counter. "I'm listening. Confused, but listening."

"That's because you're not privy to all of the delicious new details." Selene looked at Clint. "I persuaded your boy toy over here to take me back to Sal's office."

I shifted my gaze to Clint, who seemed a bit abashed. "Selene is hard to say no to."

"You hear that, Cora? I'm irresistible."

I had no idea what Selene had done to convince him but decided to let it remain a mystery for now.

"Okay, so Clint took you back to Sal's place, and I guess you broke in?"

"It wasn't hard. I found a bathroom window that was left open on the second floor."

I crossed my arms. "Uh-huh."

Selene barreled on ahead, tap-dancing across the table as she spoke, "I went through Salvatore's desk and found more letters by our mysterious scribe."

"The one about Sal's ego?" I asked.

"Bingo!" Selene stepped back and I could see letters on the table.

So, not only had she broken into Sal's place, but she'd stolen things from his desk, too. And now said letters were in my kitchen, which I think qualified me as an accessory. I shifted my gaze back to Clint. "You really went along with this? What does she have on you?"

Clint chuckled. "It seemed pretty harmless. The police didn't even have the place sealed up anymore. They're clearly not investigating further."

"So, you agree with Selene? You think he was pushed?"

Clint shrugged. "She makes a compelling argument."

Selene flashed her teeth in a self-satisfied feline grin. "You keep this up, pretty boy, and I'll make you first lieutenant when I take over the police force."

I ran a hand over my face. "Okay, so, you think these letters were written by the same person, then?"

"I don't think—I *know*," she insisted, pinning her ears back. "While I was searching, I came across a different series of letters, all signed by someone named Francine Withers. The handwriting from this group matches the threatening letter I found upon my first investigation."

"Okay, and what were all these letters about?" I prompted.

"It seems this Francine woman has been trying to cajole and wheedle Sal into naming her as his successor."

"Successor to what? From the sounds of things, Salvatore's fingers were in a lot of pies."

"Chiefly, she wanted to take his place as the head of the board of trustees, which would also entail her taking over his consulting job with the Arcane Council."

"That's awfully bold. Was Sal setting up to retire?"

"I don't know for sure, but Francine seemed to be under the impression that the council members were pressuring Sal to bring on someone to train and prepare for his eventual retirement." Selene tapped a paw against one of the letters.

"Okay, wait. Back up. Are you saying you think this Francine is the one who killed Sal? Were her letters threatening?"

"Not at first," Selene replied. "They started out quite professional in nature. Flattering, almost to the point of becoming sycophantic." Selene's eyes narrowed. "I'd definitely say that she was trying to butter him up."

"But that changed somewhere along the way?" I asked.

"They're all dated," Selene explained, "and as time went on you could tell she was growing more and more frustrated. In what she claims was her final letter, she flat out called him a disgrace to all archivists. And then, the letters stopped, up until the unsigned note."

"And when was that sent?"

"It's not dated, but if I've matched the envelope to it, it's postmarked three weeks ago. No return address."

I stepped closer to the table and inspected the pages. I didn't need to be some kind of handwriting expert to know the style matched. "As much as it pains me to admit this, Selene, it seems you could be on to something here."

Selene puffed out her chest.

I skimmed a few of the signed letters, and then gasped. "Wait a second. Francine Withers … *Frankie* Witchers." I looked up at Selene, my eyes wide. "She's the head librarian at the Winterspell Public Library."

"You're sure?"

"I never realized her full name was Francine, but look, here she refers to the stewardship she's had at the public library. There's no one else there named Francine. Just Frankie."

Selene sat down, her tail swirling through the air as she considered the new piece added to the puzzle. "So, you know our suspect, then? Does she seem the violent type?"

"Frankie?" I scoffed. "No way. She's the type who wouldn't even squish a bug. She'd trap it under a glass and then release it safely outside, rather than smash it with a heavy shoe."

"Yeah, well, people do crazy things when they think it will get them power and prestige. Morality goes out the window."

"You have a very dim view of humanity."

"No, I have a very *realistic* view of humanity."

I drummed my fingers on the table.

"What do you want to do, Cora?" Clint asked from his place in the archway between my tiny eat-in kitchen and the living room.

Straightening, I turned so I could see both him and Selene more easily. "I don't know that I believe Frankie killed Sal, but it might be worth going and speaking with her. She might let something valuable slip."

"So, now you don't believe me?" Selene groused.

I exhaled. "I think you're right in that there seems to be more to this than meets the eye. You have good points, what with the liquor, and the disarray, and now this new lead … but Frankie seems so sweet and kind-hearted."

"Uh, check out this one," Selene said, lunging at one of the letters I hadn't considered. "She compares him to a soulless, slithering cobra."

"Hmm."

Generally speaking, I thought I had a good read on people, but maybe I was wearing rose-colored glasses, just like Selene said.

Sighing, I nodded. "Okay. Tell you what, we'll go and see her tomorrow morning and see what she has to say for herself."

Selene shot me a dark look. "Why wait until then? What else are you two going to do?"

My cheeks warmed as I glanced up at Clint. "I was thinking we'd start with dinner—for *two*, and take it from there."

Clint smiled. "Sounds good to me."

"Hmm. He's quite trainable," Selene said. "I think you should hold onto this one, Cora. Don't scare him off, like you did with Roger."

We did our best to ignore the snarky cat and headed out into the evening air.

THE FOLLOWING MORNING, Selene pounced on me before my alarm clock went off. Granted, after the late night out with Clint, I'd set it a little later than usual. "Come on! We're running out of time!"

"Selene—" I groaned.

"What? It's not my fault you stayed out all night, necking in the woods!"

"Necking? What are you a hundred years old?"

The cat blinked. "Closer to four, but what's your point?"

Sighing, I accepted my fate and tossed aside my covers. "Okay, okay."

Clint arrived not too long after I rolled out of bed, coffees in hand. He also had no business looking so handsome and put together that early in the morning. I felt—and probably looked—like I was halfway undead, but he was sweet enough to compliment me as he dropped a quick kiss on my lips in greeting.

Clint offered to drive while I nursed my coffee, so I climbed into the passenger seat of his BMW. Selene jumped into my lap, then walked over my chest and onto my shoulder, digging in her claws for purchase, before launching herself into the back seat.

"Ow! Selene!" I exclaimed, grabbing for my shoulder blade.

"Next time, just give me the front seat, and we can avoid all of that unnecessary contact," she replied, not an ounce of remorse in her voice.

Clint drove us to the Winterspell Public Library, a two-story building with a faded brick exterior. It was one of the town's oldest buildings, and probably one of its most lavish, too. The town's founders, both the Winters and Spelling families, were proponents of the importance of reading, and so they had spared no expense when having it built. A pair of double doors opened to a spacious room with green and white marble floors and a wide grand staircase. A colorful children's section was on the other side of the staircase. Reference books surrounded much of the first level, with plenty of tables and clusters of comfier reading chairs interspersed throughout. The second level was reserved for adult fiction.

"I haven't been here in decades," Clint said, smiling as we walked farther into the library. "My brother and I used to come here once a week, for story hour, when we were staying at the lake house."

I took his hand and squeezed it. We hadn't talked much about his deceased brother, Seth, in the weeks since solving his murder. The brothers had been estranged for years prior to Seth's death, and as part of our investigation, we'd actually convened with Seth's spirit before he moved from the Shadow Realm to the Stardust Realm. Before crossing over, Seth had said some terrible things to his brother, and while he'd apologized for them, I knew his words still stung Clint, though as far as I could tell they were all baseless ramblings of an angry and bitter man.

"Do you do have a lot of books back home in Chicago?" I asked Clint.

Clint smiled at me. "I have one of those e-readers, now. I travel so much for work that I stopped buying paperbacks. It's not a lot of fun lugging a suitcase full of reading material onto a long flight. But now that I'm stationed here, maybe I should get back to physical books. There's nothing quite like the smell of an old book, right?"

"I'm pretty sure Cora has a whole section of stinky candles that would argue that point," Selene said as she sashayed deeper into the library.

We turned left at the base of the staircase and headed into the reference section. A lone librarian manned the check-out desk, but it wasn't Frankie. Turning, I looked at the other desk on the opposite end of the first floor and spotted her sitting at a table piled high with books. She had several others lying open in a semi-circle and was scribbling down notes as she glanced at each one in turn. I approached her and smiled. She looked up, her eyes widening with recognition.

"Cora," she said with a smile, pushing up her wire-rim glasses with a painted nail. "What a pleasant surprise."

"Hi, Frankie. How have you been?"

"I can't complain," she said with a shrug. If she were hiding the fact that she'd just killed a man, she was doing an awfully good job. She looked well rested and alert as her gaze floated past my shoulder to look up at Clint. "And who is this?"

"Oh, forgive my manners. This is—"

With a shock of panic, I realized that I had no idea how to refer to Clint. Friend? Boyfriend? Partner?

"—this is Clint. Clint, this is Frankie."

Selene cleared her throat.

"Oh, and this is Selene. You may have seen her around town."

"What a sweet kitty," Frankie said, smiling as she reached out a hand to pet Selene, which the cat promptly swatted away.

"Sorry about her," I said with a cringe. "She's hopelessly rude."

Frankie smiled as she retracted her hand and picked up her pen again. "I understand. My granny has one just like her."

Clint chuckled. "Your poor grandmother."

Selene twisted her head around to scowl up at him.

Frankie smiled. "Is there anything I can help you find?"

"Um, yes, actually," I said, adopting a somber expression. "I'm sure you saw the feature in the paper yesterday morning, about Salvatore Greco's passing?"

"Oh yes, such a shame," Frankie said. Her expression displayed restrained sympathy.

"The article was very interesting, talking about his life's work. It mentioned he has a memoir so I thought I might pop over and see about checking out a copy."

"Oh, I see." Frankie nodded. "Well, unfortunately, everyone else in Winterspell had the same idea. We only have three copies, and there's already a lengthy hold list. I'll add your name to it, though."

"Of course. I should have expected that." I offered a polite smile. "Did you happen to know Mr. Greco? It sounded like he had solid ties to the library world. I wonder who they will pick to replace him on the board of trustees for the International Magical Library Society."

Again, I watched Frankie's face for any trace of a reaction, and again I got nothing for my trouble.

"Oh, for crying out loud!" Selene groaned. "This is taking forever. Look, Frankie, we know you offed the old man, so just fess up and save us all some time. I have last night's episode of *Survivor* waiting for me on DVR. I've got money down that the busty blonde *accidentally* falls out of her bikini top at least once during the challenge to try and distract the dumb jock with the big forehead."

I slapped a hand over my face. Out of all the things I never expected to hear—let alone *wanted* to hear—come flying out of Selene's mouth ...

Frankie's eyes widened, and she sputtered something unintelligible. She stared at the cat with wide-eyed shock.

"I don't ... I mean, you aren't—what are you even saying?" she blurted at last. "I had nothing to do with Sal's death! I—I don't think anyone did. The paper didn't specify what happened, but word around town is that it was a slip and fall. An accident."

I glared down at Selene. "I'm sorry, Frankie. My familiar and I are going to have a long talk about how to behave in public."

"Yeah, we'll see how that talk goes." Selene sat back on her haunches and started cleaning her paw.

"This might all be a misunderstanding, but we believe you might have sent a not-so-nice letter to Mr. Greco," Clint said softly.

Frankie's eyes widened. "How did you—well, it doesn't matter. I have nothing to hide. Yes, I did send Sal a note a few weeks back, and yes, I was pretty steamed when I wrote it."

"What got you so upset?" Clint asked.

Frankie glanced around the section of the library, then let out a sharp exhale. "I wasn't the only one," she insisted. "I wrote it the day after he informed me that he'd named his screw-up nephew, Ernesto, as his successor on the board and in his position working for the Arcane Council."

I exchanged glances with Clint.

Selene pounced. "And when that didn't work, you went to his house in the dead of night and shoved him down the stairs!"

"Selene …" I sighed.

"I was angry, yes, but I didn't kill him," Frankie said, shaking her head vehemently. "And I can prove it, too. I was working the closing shift at the library Thursday night, and then I went out for drinks with some of my coworkers. If the police want to question me, they can ask around and verify that I was nowhere near Sal's house."

Selene cocked her head to one side, considering the woman as though she could read her mind. "All right, and if it wasn't you, then who did it?"

Frankie looked taken aback by the question, but after a moment, she drew in a shaky breath and composed herself. "*If* Sal's death was indeed a homicide, then I'd suggest going and talking to Ernesto."

"The nephew?" I asked.

Frankie gave a small nod.

I frowned. "Why Ernesto? If Sal trusted him enough to name him as his successor, it seems to suggest they had a pretty good relationship."

"Ernesto's life is a massive dumpster fire." Francine's face contorted in disgust. "He burned through his trust fund in record time, taking expensive trips and trying to impress, in his words, 'hot chicks.' He also squandered all his family connections and job opportunities, which is saying something, because being a Greco really opens up some doors. But he got tossed right back through all of them. He's been fired from the last three jobs he had because he's a drunk and makes a fool out of himself. There's a viral video of him ripping off his shirt in the middle of a board meeting and challenging the Vice President of Marketing to a jujitsu match—I should point out he's never studied jujitsu."

I blinked. "And this is who Sal wanted to take his place once he retired? Why?"

Frankie sighed. "Well, that's where it gets complicated. Salvatore never had any children, so he doted on Ernesto as if he were his own son. He defended him until the end, it seems. I suppose I should have seen it coming, but I never thought Sal would let Ernesto get anywhere near the board or the Arcane

Council. How could he not have seen that those roles are far too important to hand over to someone like Ernesto?"

Frankie paused and tossed her head. "Anyway, it wouldn't surprise me to learn that Ernesto got himself into another pickle and decided to bump the old man out of his way to start collecting all the perks of his new job."

"You think he's that callous? To kill his own uncle, a man who, as you said, loved him like a father?"

"He's a real piece of work. I personally haven't heard him say anything against his uncle, but there are more than a few stories floating around about blow-up fights between the two of them. Mostly over money. Sal gave and gave, but it was never enough for Ernesto."

I exchanged glances with Clint. It seemed as if we had a new suspect.

"Thanks for your time, Frankie," I said. "And again, I'm so sorry about Selene."

Frankie nodded, but there was a cold fire in her eyes. "I'll see you around, Cora."

My stomach twisted into a knot as we hurried away from her table and headed for the exit.

"I wonder how long it will be before Frankie

suspends your library card," Selene said. "I don't imagine she'll take too kindly to being called a murderer."

My eyes bulged. "But I didn't—you're the one who …" I heaved a sigh. "Oh, never mind."

"You know, it would be for the best if you lost your library card, anyway," Selene said.

"Why is that?" I asked with a frown.

"Because you like to read late at night, and all that squinting is only going to, ahem, shall we say exacerbate the lines around your eyes?"

"Selene!" Clint glared at Selene. "Cora does *not* have wrinkles around her eyes, or anywhere else, for that matter."

"I said what I said," the cat called over her shoulder as she stalked ahead a few paces. "You should listen to me, Cora. You can't trust a thing this guy tells you."

"I can't? And why is that?" I asked.

"Because he's liable to say anything on account of he's trying to get lucky."

"All right, let's get out of here," I groaned as I shoved the door open and let the sassy cat out of the library. "Talk like that is not exactly fit for story hour."

9

*A*fter a peaceful—AKA Selene-free—and productive Sunday at the shop, Clint took me out for dinner and a walk through town. It was late when I returned home and as I tiptoed to the kitchen to put my leftovers in the fridge, I passed Selene snoozing in a curled-up ball on the back of the couch. I smiled to myself and wondered if she'd been waiting up for me, sitting in a spot where she could keep watch out the window. She'd never admit it, of course. But maybe, just maybe, she'd missed having me around.

I put my food away and went down the hall to bed, where I promptly fell into a deep and dreamless sleep.

The following morning, I rose and fed Selene

before even *thinking* about making coffee or showering. I'd learned my lesson the hard way the other day. Dawn broke crisp and clear, with a gentle golden light that made me yearn for a trip around the lake in my kayak. Alas, duty called.

I ate a quick breakfast of cold cereal and snagged a banana and my travel mug and hit the road. I wanted to pop into the library before circling back to open Wicked Wicks. Mondays weren't terribly busy, and I figured even if I opened a little late, no one would really mind.

"Where are we going?" Selene asked when I turned the opposite direction out of the driveway. She sat in the basket affixed to the front of my bike, her usual seat for the ride to the shop.

"I thought we would stop by the library and verify Frankie's alibi. She told us she was out with her co-workers for happy hour the night Sal died. I just think we should double-check her story, and maybe see if anyone else has a lead for us."

Selene craned around to look up at me as I pedaled us along. "Aha. Thinking like a true detective. You angling for that first lieutenant job, too? I already promised it to Clint. Though, I could kick him to the curb."

I laughed. "Good to know. But I think I'll stick

with candle making. Honestly, I feel like we're getting closer to the truth about Aunt Lavender. I feel it in my gut. Whatever happened to Sal ... and the book ... I think it's connected somehow."

"Could be," Selene agreed through a slight yawn as she tipped her chin upward and enjoying the morning breeze blowing through her fur.

"The city is so quiet this time of morning," she said. "Nobody around but the prey animals. I could get used to this."

"You know, now that my shop hours are shorter, we could go out for a walk every day."

"Yeah, right. Like you'd do that."

I shrugged. "I'm still used to waking up at the same time, but now I have more time before opening. It wouldn't bother me to spend it at the lake, or just wandering through the neighborhood. I spend all day cooped up in the shop. If I don't have time to kayak, maybe I can at least get some fresh air while you do your ... cat things."

"Yeah, that might be nice. Watch the birds chirp in the trees. Maybe pick off a few of 'em. Yeah, I could get used to that kind of routine—but I hate getting up early. I'll have to think about it."

The Winterspell Public Library was eerily quiet as well. I almost cringed at the sound of my own footsteps clanging against the marble floors. A woman sat at the check-out desk on the first floor, a book in her hands.

"Excuse me," I said as I approached. "Belinda, right?"

The brown-haired woman looked up at me with sleepy green eyes. "That's right. Can I help you with something?"

"This might sound like a strange question, but did I see you and Frankie out at Merlin's Well this past Thursday? You know, Ladies Night?"

Belinda tilted her head slightly, then smiled. "Oh, I know who you are. Cora, right? You run Wicked Wicks?"

"That's me," I said with a weak smile.

"I keep meaning to stop by your shop, but who has the time?" She chuckled. "As to your question, it's possible you saw us there, but Frankie needed to go, so we left awfully early."

"Oh, that's too bad. I hope she wasn't sick. I know there's a stomach bug going around."

"No, no, nothing like that," Belinda said before heaving a sigh. "She got all upset because Ernesto Greco came into the bar. She's got a real vendetta against him and was so upset she grabbed her purse and left her drink there on the table." Belinda shrugged her narrow shoulders. "I understand where she's coming from, I suppose. She's worked really hard to get to where she's at, and thought she had this big promotion coming to her but then Ernesto got picked instead. She just can't stand the sight of him."

"And Ernesto Greco is related to that man who died recently?" I asked, still playing dumb.

To my surprise, Selene let me roll with it and didn't attempt to commandeer the conversation.

"That's right. Salvatore Greco. Ernesto is his nephew. Salvatore is the one who gave Ernesto the promotion." Belinda's expression was placid and her tone was even-keeled, so I couldn't get a sense of her personal feelings on the matter.

"So, was Frankie pretty steamed at Salvatore too, then?"

"That's an understatement. The whole situation sets her off. Normally Frankie's pretty low key. I've never seen her so much as raise her voice with someone, but at the bar that night, she walked right up to Ernesto and laid into him. I couldn't make out what she said but based on Ernesto's expression it couldn't have been good." Belinda shook her head. "I was afraid it might go further, but Gerry the bartender broke things up and told Frankie to take a walk. I didn't want Frankie to feel abandoned, so I went with her."

"What happened after that?"

"Well, I offered to drive us somewhere else, but Frankie didn't want to. She just wanted to go home."

I exchanged a meaningful look with Selene. "That's a shame. Well, maybe I'll see you both there another time."

"I'd like that," Belinda said with a smile. "And I promise I'll stop by your shop one of these days."

I returned her friendly smile as I turned to leave. "I'll see you later."

Selene and I made a quick lap around the first floor of the library, in an effort to look like we hadn't come in just to pump Belinda for information, but we quickly left and stepped out into the brisk morning air.

Selene looked up at me with a flash of teeth. "Nicely played in there."

I laughed. "Are you actually complimenting me? Wow. I might need to sit down and just take it in."

The cat swished her tail. "Don't be ridiculous," she chided. "What's our next move? That Belinda chick just torpedoed the living daylights out of Frankie's alibi."

"Not to mention, she solidified the grudge

Frankie's been holding against both Sal *and* Ernesto."
I pursed my lips in thought. "This just got a little bit more complicated. I don't want to confront Frankie again, but I also don't trust that Sheriff Templeton will take us seriously, unless we have more solid proof."

"Well, there are the letters," Selene suggested.

I raised an eyebrow at her. "Yeah, but we're not even supposed to have those, remember?"

Selene muttered a string of colorful words under her breath as we walked to the bike rack.

"Just because Frankie didn't stay out drinking all night doesn't mean she killed Salvatore. We need to verify if she made it home, and at what time."

Selene jumped up into her basket. "And how are we going to do that?"

"I think we're going to have to do some snooping," I said with a slight cringe. "Hopefully she has a nosy, chatty neighbor with lots of free time on their hands."

"Yeah, right," Selene sneered. "We both know how this is going to go down. Spoiler alert: It's going to be a big waste of time."

"Oh, ye of little faith. You know, it wouldn't hurt you to be a little bit optimistic."

"How do you know I'm not allergic to optimism?" Selene snorted. "Anyway, if we're going to do this, let's do it. You're going to be late opening up the shop at this rate."

"Since when do you give a flying fig about how my business is doing?"

"I care, so far as it affects your ability to keep paying the bill at the fish market," she replied bluntly.

"Ah. That makes a lot more sense."

"Next question, how are we supposed to find a neighbor when we don't have her address?" Selene asked.

I paused, my legs straddling my bike. "Hmm. That is a good question."

"Yes, I thought so," Selene muttered in a sarcastic tone.

"She might be listed in the Winterspell Directory," I said, scanning the street for a pay phone. They were something of a relic, but there were a handful around town mostly collecting dust in the era of cell phones.

I spotted one across the street from the library and found a mostly intact directory hanging from a bungee cable underneath the receiver. I wasn't sure how often the directory came out, but as I was looking for Frankie's information, I passed the page with my own information and noticed it was still listed as Roger Wyatt and Cora Hearth.

Ignoring the sting in my chest, I flipped through the pages trying to find the *W* section.

"Aha. Jackpot." I typed the address into my phone's GPS, and we set off. The streets were still quiet, but there were more cars hitting the road as people began their workday. Frankie's house was near the high school, a subdivision of ranch-style homes with well-tended yards and nice wide side-walks. A pack of moms, each pushing a stroller, passed by Francine's house as I came to a stop and started scouting out a potential busybody.

I found her in the form of Karen Whitman, a teacher at the school Leanna worked at, and a some-times customer of my shop.

When I first spied Karen, she was in the midst of trimming her bushes. That is to say, ostensibly trim-ming her bushes, because it looked to me like she was just standing there holding the trimmers while staring intently into the kitchen window of Frankie's house.

"Winner, winner, chicken dinner," I said.

Selene perked. "You promise?"

I pulled my bike closer to where Karen stood and

raised my hand to get her attention. "Karen? Is that you?"

Karen swung around, trimmers in hand, and broke into a wide smile. "Oh, hello, Cora!" She bustled over to the fence separating her yard from the sidewalk. "I've been meaning to come and see you. Do you still make those eucalyptus candles?"

"Absolutely," I replied. "One of my best sellers."

"Oh, good! That's a nice bike. I like your kitty, too. How sweet you two look like that!" Karen said with a chuckle.

Selene's ears flattened. She did *not* like being called cute. Fierce. Formidable. Striking. These were all acceptable. Cute, fuzzy, and adorable were all off limits.

As it turned out, Karen was not only willing to talk, but downright eager. And she had all the juicy gossip on everyone in the neighborhood. She knew that Mr. Harrison across the street had a secret family out in the non-magic world. And the woman who lived two houses down was running an illegal phoenix breeding business. Fortunately, her extensive knowledge also included useful information about Frankie.

After telling her that I was a friend of Frankie's, and had missed her at Ladies Night on Thursday,

Karen jumped in. "Oh, I thought maybe it got cancelled or something. She usually doesn't get in until well after ten or eleven on Thursdays, so I was surprised to see her come home around eight-thirty."

"Eight-thirty, huh?" I asked. "Are you sure of the time?"

"Oh yes. I had just brought my son home from a basketball game, and stayed out to water the plants before turning in. He's on the varsity team this year," she beamed.

"That's impressive," I said, flashing a quick smile. "How did Francine seem when she came home?"

"I'm sorry, I don't understand." Karen frowned. "What do you mean?"

"I mean, what was her state of mind?"

Karen's eyes dawned with the light of realization. "Oh, okay. Now that you mention it, she seemed kind of upset about something."

"What made you think she was upset?"

"Normally, Frankie comes over to say hello. She's real friendly like that. But that night, she just stormed inside, like she didn't see anything around her. I'm not sure she was even aware of her surroundings; you know what I mean?"

"Thanks so much for your time, Mrs. Whitman."

"Anytime. Just remember—"

"I didn't hear it from you." I waved goodbye and sighed. "I should have listened to my gut. I knew Frankie was too nice to kill anyone. Ugh. This has been a wild goose chase."

"Well, I wouldn't worry about that too much," Selene said. "You've got bigger problems."

"I do?"

Selene gestured over her head with the tip of her tail. "Frankie just saw us out the window and she doesn't look too happy."

"What? No …" I turned around and my heart sank. Frankie was indeed storming across her lawn, face crossed with an angry sneer.

"I can see it, but I don't believe it," Frankie fumed, storming up to us with her hands balled into fists. "First you and your nosy cat come to my place of work and accuse me of something really awful. I didn't owe you an explanation, but I answered your questions. And yet, here you are. Did you have fun interrogating my neighbors about me? Did you get all the juicy gossip from Karen?"

"Listen, Frankie, I was just trying to confirm your story—"

"Oh, I figured as much." Frankie crossed her arms over her chest and glared at me. "I thought we were friends, Cora. Maybe not good friends, but at least library friends. You should know better than this."

"I'm sorry, Frankie—"

"I don't want to hear it," she snapped. "Please, just get out of here and leave me alone. I didn't have anything to do with Sal. End of story."

"It's not so much about Sal, but rather, it's—"

"Save it," Frankie interrupted, already spinning on her heel to storm back up to her front door.

Karen was practically hanging over her fence to hear the whole exchange but had the good nature to straighten and pretend to not be listening when I kicked off the curb and pedaled away on my bike.

I could have died of embarrassment. My cheeks were hot as I hurried to get as far away from Frankie's house as I could. I was starting to wonder why I was getting involved in the case at all.

"Oh man, your face when she came up to you," Selene howled with laughter. "You were so freaked out."

"This is funny to you?" I asked the cat. "You know what? Never mind. This whole thing is stupid. I should just leave it alone and let the police figure it out. We're probably barking up the wrong tree, anyway."

"I never bark," Selene replied.

I groaned. "Don't you ever feel guilty? Don't you have even the slightest bit of a conscience?"

"Conscience? That sounds like a funny made-up human word."

"You *would* think that."

I pedaled the rest of the way to Wicked Wicks in silence, still stewing over my awkward encounter with Frankie. I opened up my shop about twenty minutes late and jumped right into work, if for no other reason than when my hands were busy, my mind tended to be at least a little quieter. I spent a good amount of the morning tending to customers and working on replenishing my depleted stock.

One thing I'll say about being busy: it makes time fly. Before I knew it, lunchtime arrived. I ordered in so I could work while awaiting the arrival of my meal. I was munching on the last bits of my Caesar salad when a teenage boy came in. I don't get a lot of teen boys in my shop, so he kind of stuck out like a sore thumb. His freckled face contorted in confusion as he looked around the shop.

"Can I help you?" I asked, setting aside my fork.

His eyes focused on me, and he strode his lanky form to the counter. "Are you Cora the candle lady?"

"That's me," I said with a chuckle. "Cora the candle lady."

"Only you would think this is a title worth being proud of," Selene muttered.

"I'm Chris Whitman. Karen is my mom. She said you were asking around about Frankie, our next-door neighbor."

I frowned. "Yes, that's right. Why?"

"After you left, I asked her who you were—" He paused and ducked his chin, "—anyways, she said you were one of Frankie's friends and were asking about Thursday night. I told her that I saw Frankie leaving her house around midnight. And my mom, er, well, she thought you might want to know."

My eyes widened. "Are you sure?"

"Oh yeah, I was in the middle of a raid on Call of Honor Mage Wars. I know it was around midnight because Noobmaster9 had to go off-line right in the middle, cause his mom's upset about his grades and caught him up past curfew. The whole team got screwed. Not that she cares." He rolled his eyes. "Anyway, after I got my face blown off by a blood-rage elf, I went to get something to eat and I saw Frankie leaving her house. I remember thinking it was weird because she looked kind of … messy. Normally, she's all put together and dressed nice."

Chris shrugged his shoulders. "That's it."

"Did you see her come back?" I asked.

"Nah. I kind of got sucked into another campaign in the game. Wound up playing all night. But her car was there in the morning."

"Okay. Well, thank you for coming down here."

Chris leaned on the counter. "So, what did she do, anyway? Sleep with your boyfriend, or something?"

Selene cackled.

I blinked. "What? No! No, no. It's nothing. I was just—"

I was just what?

I cleared my throat. "It's not a big deal. Here—" I stepped over to a display and snagged one of the eucalyptus candles. "Give this to your mom, will you?"

Chris didn't look impressed, but he took the candle and shuffled out of the shop.

My heart pounded in my chest as I watched him go.

"Seems like things are getting fishy again," Selene said behind me. "Speaking of—where's my tuna salad? Did you forget to order it?"

10

*A*s the owner and proprietor of Wicked Wicks, I'd learned long ago that I had to wear many hats. I was the CEO, the cashier, the chief shrink officer, and the customer service representative. I should point out I also manufactured the stock, which put me in a unique position as my own supplier.

And sometimes I had to act like a bouncer, or a bartender shouting out "last call" when I still had customers wandering around the shop when closing time was fast approaching.

"You know what we need?" Selene asked from her perch on the shelves behind the register.

I braced myself for her latest suggestion.

"A loudspeaker," she said. "Or one of those air

horns. You know, something to light a fire under these lollygaggers. Oooh, you know, a flamethrower really would add some pep to their steps!"

"Oh, good grief."

Move aside arachnophobia, I had a new nightmare to deal with: Selene with access to a flamethrower.

"Yeah, that's *never* going to happen," I told her.

Her eyes narrowed to slits as she scanned the remaining customers. "You're just too nice. You think these people care at all about your needs? Do you think they respect the fact that you have things to do besides wait on them hand and foot?"

I thought this was rich, considering Selene was likely two or three weeks away from demanding I carry her everywhere so her feet wouldn't accidentally step into a puddle. Heck, maybe she'd go straight to asking me to construct a gold-plated litter to cart her around in.

"I mean, look at that guy over there," she continued, zeroing in on a teen in the corner. "He hasn't even looked up from his phone the whole time he's been in here. Twenty bucks says he's just in here looking for Pokémon!"

"Selene, calm down." I shot her a glare. "You can leave anytime you'd like, remember?"

She leaped out onto the counter and caught the attention of a woman shopping through the clearance baskets. "You don't have to go home, but you can't stay here—"

I grabbed her before she could finish and hauled her into the back room, getting a couple of scratches on my hands for my trouble. "Knock it off!" I hissed. "We had an agreement, remember? When I took you in as my familiar, you promised you wouldn't heckle my customers. I get it, you're clearly hangry, and I'm sorry I forgot your tuna at lunchtime, but this is ridiculous."

Selene glared up at me. "Oh, that's not a shocker. You probably would have ordered it wrong anyway."

I planted my hands on my hips and leaned over her. "Can't you be nice? Ever?"

"I could be, yes, but what would the point of that be? People would start expecting me to be nice all the time, and then they'd walk all over me. Y'know, like they walk all over you?"

I bristled. "People do not walk all over me."

"Oh yeah? What about those customers out there?"

"Selene, they literally pay my bills—*your* bills!"

"Okay, and what about Roger? Always coming in here, even though you told him you just want to be friends. He certainly doesn't pay your bills, so what's your excuse there?"

"I—he—" I slammed my mouth closed. "That's different."

"Uh-huh."

"Listen, I'd rather error on the side of courtesy than be mean spirited like you."

"Mean spirited?" Selene's mouth gaped open. "Is that really what you think of me?"

I felt a stab of guilt, but I was too worked up to give in to it. "Yes, yes it is."

"Oh, well thank you! But flattery will get you nowhere. The fact is, you need me. You need me to be the bad guy, so you can point at me and say 'hey, look, there goes the bad guy—'"

"Selene, you're quoting *Scarface* again, and I don't need you to be the bad guy."

"Yes, you do. You're all sugar and spice, and everything nice. 'Oh, look at me, I'm Cora. Oh fooey, I burned the darn muffins. Oh, look at my pretty little candle that will make you dream of Tom Cruise sweeping you away on a moonlit cruise—"

"First of all, I don't sound like that. My voice sounds nothing like that."

"Like what?"

"Like a pixie popping helium pills! And secondly,

I'm not a pushover. I stand up for myself. I just pick my moments. I'm not like you, snapping and sniping at everyone. But if someone crosses a line with me, I let them know."

"Uh-huh."

"You know what, I don't need this today." With a growl of frustration, I turned my back on the cat and went out to help the last of my customers.

Selene sulked in the back room and glared at me when I hit the lights and joined her again, deposit envelope in hand. "Feeling better now?" I asked.

"No. But at least you're done piddling around."

I closed my eyes and counted to three, desperate to regather my last shreds of patience.

"Come on," Selene said, "let's get going. We need to go to Lavender's house and see if we can find that book."

"Happy, happy, joy, joy," I muttered, and instantly regretted it. The truth was, I wanted to look for the book. I wanted to find my aunt.

I just wished I could have one night of quiet. If I was lucky, my earbuds were somewhere in the bottom of my purse.

Selene harrumphed. "Fine, be that way. I guess I don't *have* to tell you what I found out about Ernesto while you were peddling candles."

I quirked an eyebrow. "You heard something about Ernesto?"

"I did."

"Oh, come on, Selene. Just spit it out. Please?"

"I went down to that disgusting bar, and spoke with the owner, Gerry. You know him?"

I nodded. Gerry was a Scotsman who'd run Merlin's Well for decades. He was a hard-looking man, but everyone knew he had a heart of gold. "What did he say? You were good, weren't you?"

Selene ignored my question. "Gerry didn't want to speak ill of a customer, but there was this other old geezer there at the bar, and he said that Ernesto only has one setting when it comes to drinking: black-out drunk. He told me that Gerry has to cut him off most nights and call him a cab before he gets that way, and on more than a few occasions, Ernesto swiped bottles of liquor and poured himself an extra finger or two when Gerry's back was turned."

"Oh boy." I shook my head. "That's actually pretty sad, don't you think?"

"His wife seems to think so. This guy had all the dirt. Says Ernesto and his wife argue like all the time, too, mostly about him being a worthless drunk and drinking away all their money."

"I can see why that would put some strain on

their relationship, but why would he go around telling people all of the painful details of his personal life like that?"

"Um, hello. What part of *drunk* are you not understanding?" Selene scoffed.

"I guess." I was struck with a sudden idea. "Say, could we do what we did with Clint's brother and hold a seance? Maybe we'll have more luck this time, and Sal will remember what happened that night."

"It won't work," Selene replied.

"Why not?"

"A seance doesn't work if the soul has already crossed over to the Stardust Realm."

"And how do you know he's already crossed over?"

"Look, spirits only linger in the Shadow Realm when they feel like they have unfinished business. A guy like Salvatore has done like everything, climbed every mountain, conquered every challenge. Plus, he's old. The older the being when they pass, the more likely they are to cross over directly to the Stardust Realm. Combine those two factors, and it's pretty much a foregone conclusion that our boy Salvatore Greco is already in another realm."

"I see. But wouldn't it be worth it to try? If it doesn't work, it doesn't work, but talking to Salvatore would go a long way toward narrowing down the search for his killer. Assuming he was killed in the first place," I added, which I still wasn't sure about.

Selene sighed. "We would need a sample of his closest living relative's blood. The profile in the *Gazette* said he was leaving behind a nephew. No mention of siblings."

I bobbed my head. "So, we'd have to get Ernesto's blood?"

"Yes, exactly."

"That would be an awkward conversation," I said with a cringe.

"Ya think?" Selene followed me into the alley behind the shop and hopped into her basket. "On top of that, if Frankie's hunch was right, and Ernesto has something to do with this, I doubt he'd be willing to participate in the ritual."

"That's a good point."

"Of course, it's a good point. I just made it!"

"Okay." I frowned as I got on the bike. "Let's not start arguing again."

"Why not? I'm quite good at it," Selene replied with a flash of her dainty teeth.

WE POKED around in Lavender's so-called research library, trying to find Obin's tome, but after two frustrating hours I gave up and sat down on the floor.

"This is hopeless, Selene. If the book is here, I don't think we're ever going to find it."

The cat swished her tail as she took one more slow walk around the room, jumping from book to book, before landing on the desk. Peering down at me, she sighed. "I suppose we could go and speak with Ernesto directly, get his side of the story. See if he has an alibi for the night his uncle died."

"You really think he'll talk to us? With Frankie it was easy enough—well, until you started spouting all that nonsense about *Survivor*, anyway."

"Hey, I won that bet, thank you very much. I got fifty cold smackeroos from Bart over at the fish market."

I stared up at the cat. "You were serious? How do you even have money to gamble with?"

Selene flashed her teeth. "Well, *I* don't, but *you* do."

With a groan, I flopped back against a stack of books. "You're going to be the death of me. Or at least the thing that sends me to bankruptcy court."

"Nonsense!" Selene exclaimed, leaping through the air before landing on the books behind me. "I won you double your money, if anything, you should be thanking me!"

"Naturally." I pushed up to my feet. "Come on, let's get going. Any chance you know where Ernesto lives?"

"Oh, yes. Lavender dragged me to his place when he hosted a birthday party for Sal a few years back. He lives out in Rolling Pine Hills," she said with a shudder.

"What's wrong with Rolling Pine Hills? That's a nice neighborhood."

"Oh come on, Cora! It's like the most generic, cookie-cutter, yuppie-infested suburban nightmare ever. Straight out of the *Stepford Wives* only somehow worse because we live in a magical town, and things should just be more interesting than that by default." The cat scoffed as she stalked out of the Lavender's guest room.

"One, I think you're exaggerating. And two, I think they're called *hipsters*, not yuppies these days."

"Not even close on either account. I'm not exaggerating, and hipsters are not synonymous with yuppies."

"Then what are hipsters? I get this mental image of beards and flannel shirts and coffee shops—"

"Okay, take the anti-establishment bent of the hippies, and then add in the unaffected air of snobbery of an Ivy League legacy kid." Selene snickered. "Poof! You've got a hipster."

"I don't get it."

"Well, let's take magic, for instance. The yuppie witch has a great collection of high-end brooms, wands, cauldrons, etc. They're quite annoying and brag about their possessions constantly. A hipster witch, on the other hand, was into magic waaaaay before you were, bro, and they're soooooo over it now. See the difference?"

"They both sound equally annoying," I muttered, though I wasn't at all sure if Selene had a point or not. Personally, I tried to avoid boxing people into categories. I had wealthy friends, not-so-wealthy friends, friends who liked yoga and hiking, and friends who preferred the great indoors. People were just people to me, all shapes and sizes and colors.

"In any case, it doesn't really matter what neighborhood they live in," I said, hopefully putting an end to the weird side conversation.

We drove to Rolling Pine Hills, which as Selene said, was one of those newer developments where the Home Owners Association likely wielded more power than the goddess herself, judging by the artfully kept shrubbery, meticulously groomed lawns, and spotless streets. The sidewalks and drive-ways were a uniform tan, nary a crack in sight, and as we approached the Greco home, I had no doubt that if I were to take a level and lay it across the blades of grass in their front yard, the bubble would land dead center between the middle lines.

The homes were all huge and nice, but it wasn't a place I personally would consider. For one, it was way too far from the water, and I also didn't relish the idea of ever living someplace where the simple mistake of leaving your trash bins out overnight could land you a citation.

"What should I say?" I asked Selene as we stepped onto the Grecos' front porch.

"Seems like you should have figured that out before we got here," Selene said as she plopped her rear end on the welcome mat.

Before I could gather my thoughts and come up with a strategy, the front door swung open and a tired-looking middle-aged brunette appeared, her eyes going wide. "Who are you? If you're with the high school choir, I already donated at the car wash two weekends back."

"Um. No," I said, slightly taken aback. Did she think I was a teenager? Sure, I was short, but I didn't look like a child.

"What kind of seventeen-year-old has crow's feet?" Selene asked the woman.

The woman recoiled, surprised by the talking cat.

I delivered a gentle (ish) kick to Selene's fuzzy rear for the crack about the crow's feet.

"I'm not with the school," I told the woman. "I'm looking for Ernesto Greco. Is he home?"

"What do you want with Ernesto?" Her gaze turned more hostile as she zeroed in on me. She raised one hand and revealed a slim cigarette. Lighting it, she shuffled out onto the porch, silently forcing Selene and me to take a few steps back to make space.

"I have reason to believe his uncle, Salvatore, was murdered, and I was hoping to speak with Ernesto to see if he might have information for me."

Her eyes narrowed to slits as she took a long drag from the cigarette. "Is that so? And what are you, press? Police? Some distant relative of Sal? Huh?"

She didn't seem surprised by the suggestion that Sal's death may have involved foul play. "I'm not any of those things, no," I said, wishing I'd come up with a better cover story. Or *any* cover story, for that matter. Maybe I should have just lied and said I was with the paper. At least then I'd have a reason to be there on her front porch, poking around for information.

"Hey, Mickey, who is that? The guy from the insurance company?" a male voice called from inside the house.

The woman turned around to address the speaker. "No, some girl who thinks your uncle was murdered."

I cringed at the bluntness in her statement.

"Murdered? Well, let her in. I'd like to hear what she has to say."

The woman rolled her eyes, but she stepped back from the door. "Please, by all means, come inside."

"Thank you, uh, Mickey—" I said.

"Michelle," she snapped.

"Oh, sorry, Michelle."

I stepped past her and laid eyes on a man sprawled out in a Lazy Boy recliner, with beer in one hand and a huge plastic bowl of chips on his lap. The Greco home had a den, or office space, directly to the right of the entryway, and it seemed to have been turned into Ernesto's man cave judging by the sports memorabilia hanging from the walls, the massive flat-screen TV, and the pair of lounger chairs.

As for Ernesto himself, he didn't stand out to me in any way. He shared some common features with his uncle but had none of his uncle's poise or polish. Granted, it would be hard for even James Bond to look suave if he had a beer belly and a mess of potato chip crumbs enmeshed in his mat of dark chest hair.

"So, you think my uncle might have gotten himself offed?" He took a swig of beer and belched loudly. His hairy toes wriggled against the carpet as he waited for my response.

"Whew. Forget what I said about yuppies," Selene told me.

"Shh, quiet, Selene." I turned to address Ernesto. "I'm so sorry for your loss."

He inclined his head, then grabbed another fistful of chips.

"Um, but yes, I do think maybe he was *pushed* down the stairs," I said hesitantly.

"I wouldn't be surprised. Some of his *customers* could be a little scary. They look all harmless in their tweed suits, or whatever, but I tell you, some of them can get pretty cutthroat when it comes to rare books and other artifacts." Ernesto shuddered. "A bunch of creeps, if you ask me."

I took another step into the room. "So, you think that if anyone was going to kill Salvatore, it would have been over a book deal?"

"I don't know," Ernesto said. "The cops said it was all an accident. Sal got into some top-shelf bourbon and took a tumble."

I couldn't help but feel a little repulsed by his lack of emotion.

"What makes you think he was killed?" Michelle interjected from her place in the doorway. "Did the police change their minds and open an investigation?"

"No. At least, not yet." I heaved a sigh. I'd dipped a toe in the water, I may as well jump all the way in.

"Who are you?" Michelle asked, crossing her arms over her ample chest. "You haven't even given us your name."

"My Aunt Lavender was a friend of Sal's—"

"Lavender?" Ernesto repeated, squinting at me. When his eyes widened, he smiled. "I can see that. You sort of look like her. What's the old bird up to these days? Last time I saw her she was talking about going to Greece to find Athena's hairpin, or something silly."

My heart jumped. "When was that?"

"Oh, er, two … maybe three years ago." Ernesto shrugged and took another swig from his beer can.

My hopes deflated.

"What does that have to do with Sal?" Michelle asked. "So, your aunt is a friend. I don't see why you're poking your nose around in any of this, asking my husband all these questions."

"Yeesh, Mickey, she's just a kid. Go easy on her," Ernesto said. Then he held up his beer can and jiggled it. "What do you say you get me another one of these?"

Michelle glared at her husband, nostrils flaring. Abruptly, she turned to me. "If you want to know who had it in for Sal, you might want to go yank August Nell's chain."

"August Nell?" Ernesto repeated, his large brow furrowed. "He's one of the old man's best customers. Why would he want to kill him?"

Michelle huffed. "It's just something I overheard a few days ago at the Witch Doctors Without Borders charity auction."

Ernesto struggled to sit up a little higher in his recliner. "What did he say, Mickey?"

"I think it had something to do with Sal having a book he promised to August, and not handing it over like he was supposed to. He kept saying Salvatore was 'holding out' on him. It sounded pretty serious."

"Huh. Still, a guy like August Nell, he could buy a whole library full of books," Ernesto said. "The guy is a bona fide millionaire. He's the one who built the Winterspell Chalet. He's big in real estate."

That's why the name had sounded familiar.

Michelle tossed her hands up. "Hey, you wanted information, and now you've got it," she said before stalking down the hall, presumably toward the kitchen.

"I'm sorry about my wife," Ernesto said once she'd gone. "She's been temperamental ever since Uncle Sal died. He treated her like a princess. I'm sure you can understand."

I smiled reassuringly. "Of course. I'm sure none of this is easy on you guys. Not only are you grieving, but word on the street is you're the one who has to fill Sal's shoes now that he's gone. I imagine it's quite daunting to take on the role of the Arcane Council's archivist."

He shrugged. "Eh, I'm not one to let stuff stress me out. I figure I'll learn how to do it as I go. You know, go with the flow? Improvise? I've read that the most brilliant minds improvise most of the time. Well, I don't really read, but someone else read it and told me about it. I think it was on a podcast, or something."

I cocked an eyebrow. I was starting to see why there had been so much outrage at his posthumous promotion.

Ernesto's brow furrowed in thought. "You know, my uncle had meetings with the bigwigs at the Order every Thursday night. You might want to ask them and see if anything was off that night. My uncle was a pretty diplomatic guy, but even he had a limit. Maybe they know someone who wasn't happy with him."

"On Thursday? You weren't at the meeting, too? I thought you were sort of, in training?"

"Hey, I was probably supposed to be there for some reason or another, but nobody told me the exact time, right? So I met up with some buddies down at Merlin's Well instead. I should have known something was wrong with Sal when he didn't call me the next morning to yell at me for missing the meeting." Ernesto ducked his chin and stared down into the bowl of chips for a long moment.

"Again, I'm so sorry for your loss." I took a step backward. "Thank you for your time, Ernesto."

As I was slipping out the door, Michelle was stomping down the hall, a cold beer in hand. She gave me an irritated look and I hustled to close the door shut behind me.

As we walked to the car, Selene looked up at me. "Whew. Those two are really in the running for America's sweethearts, aren't they?"

I shrugged. "Maybe not, but Ernesto seemed pretty sincere to me. What do you think about his story? You already verified his alibi. He was at the bar that night. Frankie's story puts him there, too."

"Strike two," Selene said.

Exhaling, I paused and unlocked the car. "So, I guess now we need to look into August Nell."

Selene smiled. "Oh, sure. I mean, how hard could it be to get a meeting with a literal millionaire to ask if he's some kind of cold-blooded killer? This should be a piece of cake."

11

*C*lint had dinner plans with his mother, so it was just me and Selene at the house that evening. In some ways, I was losing track of what it was like to live alone. Before Selene, I spent the majority of my nights in silence, killed only by turning on the TV to whatever I could find that was halfway interesting. It wasn't that I'd minded being on my own, but now that I had company, I realized that maybe I'd been lonelier than I'd been willing to admit, even to myself.

As I sat down on the couch beside Selene to watch one of her favorite shows, I couldn't help but smile at the contented look on her face. Maybe we'd both been lonely. My aunt Lavender meant well, but she didn't make for good company most of the time.

She lived too much in her own head and tended to forget about those around her—Selene included.

Of course, my sympathetic and sentimental thoughts quickly vanished in the morning light when I awoke to the persnickety cat sitting on my chest, caterwauling a song of her own invention:

"Hey, I wrote a song for you, Cora. It's called … there's no food in my bowl! I'm starving. Look at me, I'm skin and bones, but you lay there lazy as a toad, a tooooad!"

I glared at her from above the seam of my coverlet. "That doesn't rhyme, and nobody's getting fed until I go to the bathroom. Maybe next time, try not using my bladder as your own personal trampoline."

Afterward, I stumbled about the kitchen, feeding Selene and getting the coffee pot going. It wasn't much, but it was our little routine.

"You're really going to the shop again today?" Selene asked when she finished noshing on her fancy cat food.

I glanced up from my bowl of oatmeal. "Of course."

"Ugh. I think you should read this book, it's called *The Four-Hour Workweek*."

I arched a brow. "Oh, yeah? Does it have a winning lottery ticket stuffed in the pages somewhere? Because if not, I don't think something like that would be of much help."

Selene paced the length of the kitchen, her tail swishing in time with her ranting. "Look, all I'm saying is that you should live a little. All this work, work, work … it's exhausting!"

I couldn't help but smirk. "Okay, and which part is exhausting for you? For the most part, you just nap in whatever part of the shop is getting the best sunlight."

The cat stopped and peered up at me. "Would it blow your mind if I said I was worried about *you?*"

I blinked. "Actually, yeah. It kind of would."

I lifted a hand to the side of my head and made an explosion gesture, complete with sound effects.

Selene swirled away from me and stalked out of the room, muttering under her breath.

I smiled and shoveled a bite of oats into my mouth.

Despite Selene's lecture, there was work to be done. I couldn't wave a magic wand and replenish my stock, make sales, and clean. If only. But as I went about the day, I did wonder if maybe I was at the place where I could justify having a full-time employee. During the summer, I usually hired one or two college students to help with the busiest season.

They left to go back to school at the end of August, as things were slowing down. It had worked well so far, but then my life had grown more complicated in the past months. I had a … well, a Clint. I still wasn't sure how to categorize him. Then there was Selene. My patchy social life, most of which revolved around Leanna, book club, and Thursday nights at Merlin's Well. I also had my family dinners every other Tuesday night.

It all left precious little time for anything outdoorsy. Kayaking, hiking, swimming, star gazing.

Maybe I should release a little of the pressure before things boiled over.

It was a quarter to ten when Clint's BMW pulled into the parking spot nearest Wicked Wicks' door. I hadn't been expecting him, and quickly brushed a hand through my still damp hair. I glanced down at Selene. "How do I look?"

"Haggard, worn out, clearly not the first pick at dodgeball or the school dance—"

"Never mind," I snapped.

I forced a smile as Clint turned and used his shoulder to push open the door, as his hands were full of pastries and coffee.

"Good morning," he said, stopping long enough to peck me on the lips. His kiss felt warm and wonderful. The smoothness of his recently shaven cheek, the sultry notes of his expensive cologne, and his general manliness combined to make my head spin just a little.

"Good morning. Did you bring me breakfast again? You've got to stop doing that."

"Why?" He asked with a laugh, laying his burdens down on the sales counter.

"Because Spanx can only do so much," Selene quipped.

I glared at Selene. "You know what? I'm going to enjoy my pastries, and if you say one more nasty thing to me this morning, I'm going to whip you away in a tornado so big you'll be lucky if you ever come back down again. I hope you like living in the land of Oz."

Selene scampered off into the stock room. Just in case she got any ideas about returning, I sent a gust of wind after her and slammed the door shut behind the cat's loping form.

"She knows better than to tempt fate," I muttered under my breath.

"Hey, don't sweat what that cat says. You're a very beautiful woman, Cora."

I turned my gaze down toward the floor, feeling my cheeks flush. "You don't have to say that."

"Have to?" Clink chuckled and shook his head. "No, there's no *have to* about it. I'm just out here stating the facts."

"Well, then I'm a lucky lady," I said, looking up through my lashes to meet his eyes. They were dark brown and always seemed to have a little gleam of sparkle in them.

We kissed again, before settling in for our tasty treats. The pastries were delicious, though Clint somehow managed to buy every flavor but my favorite. There was tangy lemon, rich blueberry, and sweet cherry, but no cream cheese. I happen to think cream cheese pastries, when done correctly, are an art form unto themselves, transcending their more mortal kin.

Which isn't to say that I didn't demolish the pastries Clint did bring. I'm not saying that at all. The coffee was the perfect contrast, a South American blend with bold, darkly roasted flavor and a hint of cinnamon without any cloying sweetness.

The bitter yet flavorful coffee was a great chaser to the sweet pastries. I was wiping my fingers on a napkin and considering the last swallow in my paper cup when the bells hanging over the front entrance jingled.

Clint and I both glanced up as a good-looking

man in his early thirties strolled in. He stood about the same height as Clint, but was easily twenty pounds heavier, all of it muscle and broad shoulders. His expertly manicured beard and rugged sense of style made him look as if he'd stepped off the page of a Cabela's catalog.

He was my ex-husband, Roger. And he too came bearing gifts.

"Hey, Cora," he said, barging in, his gaze focused on the packages in his arms more than what was transpiring inside my shop. "I know this is sudden, but I was at Sugar Shack getting some treats, and I remembered how much you loved cream cheese pastries and so I thought, you know, what the heck, why not surprise her—"

He looked up at last and froze dead in his tracks when he saw Clint standing there. Roger's gaze darted from Clint to my face, to the pastry remnants of our breakfast repast, and back through the whole cycle again.

"Except that you're already having breakfast, with Clint. Hello, Clint."

"Hello, Roger," Clint said, flashing an awkward smile.

I could have died from the awkwardness. It reminded me of the very first night that I'd met

Clint. I'd been in the midst of closing up when he stopped in, looking for a gift for his mother. I'd wisely steered him away from the spicy dreams candle he'd been carrying around in his hands, and somewhere along the way, he'd asked me to dinner. And then Roger had waltzed through the door. Awkwardness ensued, and Clint had gone running for the hills before I could give him a definitive answer about his dinner invitation.

What can I say, the man has impeccable timing.

Roger cleared his throat. "Uh, I guess I should have called ahead, huh?" He forced a laugh before depositing the bag on the counter. "Ah, here you go. You two should, um, enjoy those … I'll just be going."

"Are you sure you don't want them?" Clint asked, gesturing at the bag.

"He's—"

"I'm—"

"—lactose intolerant," we both finished, in stereo.

Roger smiled at me. "What she said."

With a laugh, he headed for the door.

"Thanks for thinking of me," I told him.

Roger cast one last, longing look over his shoulder before he departed.

We'd been divorced for eighteen months, and for most of that, had lived in different cities. Different worlds, really, as he'd opted to leave Winterspell and the magic world entirely and strike out into the non-magical world. But when his burgeoning start-up crashed and burned, he'd returned to home, and to my bewilderment, seemed to be under the impression that he and I could pick up where we'd left off. I didn't want to get romantically entangled with my ex, but there was still a mutual love and respect that made it hard for me to tell him to kick rocks.

"So," Clint said, opening the bag that Roger left. "Cream cheese is your favorite, huh? I never knew."

"You never asked," I blurted. I hadn't intended it to be mean, but Clint winced. "I mean, I should have just told you. You're not a mind reader," I said, smiling to recover the moment. "I mean, unless you are and you just haven't told me yet."

"No, you're right. I should have asked." He shrugged. "These do look tasty. You want a bite?"

"No, thank you, my tummy is stuffed already. You go right ahead."

He rolled the top of the bag down again without taking a pastry. "That's okay. You keep them for tomorrow. I'd bet they're great after a few minutes in the toaster oven." He grinned, trying to make the situation feel less awkward. After a second, he checked his watch. "Um … I hate to eat and run, but I need to get going too."

"Oh yeah? Another big-time business deal?"

"Not this time. I'm actually meeting with one of the local real estate agents about finding a rental property. Have you heard of the Farrow brothers?"

"Yeah. I think they might be the only real estate agents in Winterspell," I said with a laugh. "They helped me—er, well, me and Roger, when we bought the—my house."

Clint nodded. "Right. Well, I'm hoping they can help me out. My mother's lakeside estate might be four-thousand square feet, but somehow still feels claustrophobic right now."

I gave a sympathetic nod. Taking care of a dying person had to be one of the hardest, saddest jobs imaginable. I didn't blame him one bit for wanting a place of his own to get away from it all.

"So, this rental … long- or short-term lease?" I dared to ask.

"We'll see what they can do," he said with a half-cocked grin as he raised a hand and left the shop.

I worked throughout the day unsure of what to make of Clint's comment. If he was going through the trouble of finding a rental, it seemed natural to assume he was planning on staying in Winterspell for the foreseeable future, otherwise why go through the trouble? And if all he wanted was a crash pad, surely with his money he could afford a suite at the Winterspell Chalet and stay in style. A rental was a commitment. But it didn't mean it was a commitment to me.

Selene kept to herself after our little battle that morning, and I wondered if she would come back to the shop before I closed up. I wasn't going straight home after work. It was Tuesday and I had standing dinner plans at my mom's house.

I about stepped on the cat when I went to take out the trash. "Selene!" I exclaimed, jumping back. "You're going to get one or both of us killed! What are you doing out here on the step?"

The cat lazily rolled to her other side, showing off her belly. "Catching some rays," she said.

Scoffing, I made a show of stepping *over* her, took the trash to the dumpster, and then brushed my hands off on my apron before pulling it off and folding it into a loose square. "Come on. It's family dinner night. I assume you're tagging along?"

That got her to her feet. "Ooh, do you think Lilac made her crab puffs again this time?"

I smiled as I locked the back door. "Guess we'll have to go find out."

We drove across town to my mom's house, and made our way inside, not bothering to knock. It wasn't the house where I'd spent my childhood, but it still felt like home to me.

Mom was in the dining room, laying plates out around the table. "Hey!" I greeted. "Can I help with anything?"

I frowned and counted the plates. There was an extra setting. "Are we having company tonight? Oh my gosh, do you have a *date*?"

Mom scoffed. "Absolutely not. You know I'm not interested in dating."

I sighed. "I know that you *say* that, but I secretly think maybe one day you'll bump into Mr. Wonderful in the paper towel aisle at the market, or wind up going on a blind date with a handsome stranger when there's only one table left at Dragon's Gold."

Mom laughed. "Oh, Cora. You should write books. You have quite a mind for fiction!" She set down the last set of silverware, then clasped her hands together and smiled at me. "Besides, don't you already know who's coming to dinner? He was supposed to tell you."

"He? He who?"

"Why, Roger, of course! He said he was going to drop by the shop today and let you know."

I flinched. Roger's little impromptu visit suddenly made a lot more sense.

Selene cackled. "You should see your face, Cora!"

Mom smiled. "It's just a dinner, Cora. It will be fine."

"How—how did this even happen?"

"We ran into each other at the movie theater yesterday afternoon. We were both *flying solo*, as the kids say, and so we sat together and got to talking during the previews. He mentioned how much he's missed my cooking, so I thought, to heck with it, why not invite him over!"

"I could think of about a dozen reasons, chief among them being that he's your daughter's ex-husband." I rubbed one hand over my head. My hair had air-dried and lay flat against my head without the help of a spritz of product.

"It will be fine, Cora," Mom said, already sashaying into the kitchen with Selene hot on her heels.

"Any chance you made those crab puffs?" Selene asked, before glancing over her shoulder to snicker at me.

12

*I*n this corner: Cora Hearth weighing in at … well, never mind—she's a specialist in creating magical candles and getting involved with indecisive men. In the opposite corner: Lilac Hearth, Cora's stubborn-as-a-mule mother, AKA the Irresistible Force.

Ding ding. Round one.

"Mom, you can't keep interfering in my life like this," I said, following her into the kitchen as she checked the contents of the oven. The smell that poured out of it was so delectable I almost got derailed.

"How am I interfering? It's my house, my dinner, and my chorizo-stuffed chicken, and I'll invite whoever I want over for dinner." My mother straightened up and doffed her oven mitts. "Needs about eight more minutes."

"You seriously don't think this is weird? Inviting my ex to dinner?" I said in an exasperated growl.

"He's your ex, but he's also a dear friend of mine. I didn't stop being friends with him just because the two of you divorced. He was good to you, Cora. He was good *for* you, too, if you ask me."

"Yeah, well, I'm not. And I don't appreciate you making it sound like I did something wrong or drove him away. We're both adults. We made our choices."

Mom stopped and braced one hand on the edge of the counter. "And which one of you brought up the D word?" she asked.

My mouth dropped open. "You *cannot* be serious right now. Also, pot-kettle much? *You're* divorced, too! What would you say if I invited Dad over to one of these family meals? Would that be just peachy keen?"

"Drats! I need popcorn. Or, maybe popcorn chicken," Selene quipped as she watched us like we were in a verbal tennis match.

Mom's eyes blazed with heat, and a flare of sparks shot from her fingertips. She jerked her hand away from the counter and extinguished the flames she'd conjured. "That would be a little hard to do, seeing as he's across the country. I also don't think his little Pop Tart and their three brats would approve."

I cringed. Bringing my dad into this was a mistake. Truth be told, I didn't have much of a relationship with him beyond the annual birthday and Christmas card exchange.

"Okay, okay. Maybe that's not the same thing," I conceded. "But still, didn't you even think about asking me if I would be okay with this?"

Mom pursed her lips, then exhaled, and some of the fight drained from her eyes. "I guess it didn't occur to me that you would mind. Maybe I missed something along the way, but I thought you said you and Roger were trying to be friendly since he's returned to town. Your divorce was night and day compared to me and your father."

She crossed to the stove and tasted a green bean and potato concoction burbling on the stove. Her brow furrowed, and she used spellwork to cause the saltshaker to take flight and sprinkle over the pot.

"All I meant by that is that we smile at each other in public, and yes, he's stopped by the shop a time or two—"

"A time or *two?*" Selene sputtered.

I shot her a death glare. "Stay out of this."

"Okay, well what would you like me to do, Cora? Should I call him and tell him he's uninvited?"

And your winner by a TKO in the first round, Lilac Hearth, AKA the irresistible force.

Sighing, I held up my hands in surrender. "It's fine. We can get through one meal, but please, let's keep things casual and not make this a regular thing, all right?"

Selene scoffed. "Typical."

My brother, Evan, came in the side door and looked between me and Mom. "Whoa, what's going on in here?"

Mom slapped a sweet smile on her face. "Nothing at all, sweetie." She pecked him on the cheek as he leaned his tall frame in for a hug. "How have you been?"

"Emme lost her first tooth yesterday at the park. She got a visit from the Tooth Fairy, and now I think Ruby is trying to knock one of her teeth out so she can be just like sissy," he said with an exasperated sigh. "So, if either of you catch them going after the other with a croquet mallet, please intervene."

I couldn't help but giggle at the visual. My twin nieces were a handful on the best of days, but when they teamed up for a shared mission: look out world!

"Something smells amazing," Evan said, bending over to take a peek inside the oven.

Mom playfully slapped him away. "A few more minutes. Why don't you get the girls washed up?"

Evan pulled a face but laughed as he headed out of the kitchen to round up his family.

"Now, Selene, I know it's not quite what you expected, but I think you'll like it. It's a recipe I picked up from that cranky British chef, the one who makes people cry."

"Gordon Ramsay," I supplied.

"Hmm, no, not him. He's a blond fellow, spiky haircut, likes to curse a lot. Had a show called, uh, what was it ... *Hell's Kitchen*! I think that's it."

"Yes, that's Gordon Ramsay, Mom," I said, a bit annoyed.

"No, no, that doesn't sound right. His name sounds like May ... that's it, Bobby Slay."

"Bobby *Flay*, Mom, and he's a totally different guy than Gordon Ramsay."

"No, I'm pretty sure it's Bobby Slay."

I grabbed my phone. "Look, I'm going to show you a picture of Gordon Ramsay, and you tell me if it's the guy you're thinking of."

A knock came at the door, and I froze. Roger. It had to be Roger ...

I ran my hand over my hair once more.

Evan's voice sounded from the front room. "This feels like a flashback!" he said with a jovial laugh. "How's life treating you, man?"

"Can't complain," Roger replied. "How about you? The girls are getting so big!"

Evan laughed again. "Tell me about it. They just started kindergarten if you can believe it. I swear, I need a pause button."

Evan poked his head in the kitchen, wearing a huge grin as he met my eyes. "Did I miss something? Are you two back together again or something?"

"Mother, Maiden, and Crone, I sincerely hope there is wine around here somewhere."

Roger wore a pair of designer jeans and a charcoal turtleneck. His face creased in a smile when he saw me. "No, we're just friends."

"Oh." Evan sounded slightly deflated. Who knew my *entire* family was on Team Roger? It was certainly news to me.

I grabbed a corkscrew and a bottle of merlot and headed into the dining room.

Roger followed me and grabbed at my elbow. "Cora, is it okay that I'm here?" he asked, keeping his voice hushed.

I set the bottle on the table and started attacking

the cork. "Does it matter what I say? You're here. Let's just ... get ... through ... this—"

"Here," Roger said, taking the bottle from me as I struggled to get the cork free. He popped it out without so much as a flinch, then handed me the bottle. "I'm sorry. I wanted to tell you this morning, but—"

Nodding, I poured myself a generous serving of the red wine. "I know. Clint was there."

"Are you two ... um ... getting serious?"

"I don't know." I shook my head, then gulped from my wine glass. "It's new, you know? I haven't done this since—well, since you and me were ... you and me."

Roger gave me a solemn nod. "Right."

My mother swept into the dining room from the kitchen, bearing a steaming bowl of green bean and potato medley. Behind her, Evan struggled to keep the heavy roast chicken from sliding off the sterling silver platter.

Ruby and Emme bounded into the room and each clung to one of my legs, nearly sending my wine sloshing all over their adorable little heads. Roger swooped in and saved the wine, taking the glass from my hand, our fingers touching for the briefest of moments.

"Thank you," I told him, before leaning over to put my face level with my nieces. "I hear someone met the Tooth Fairy!"

Emme pulled her lips away from her teeth in a slightly crazed looking smile to show off the gap in her front teeth.

"I'm going to be next, Auntie Cora!" Ruby declared with gusto.

I kissed her on the forehead. "Don't be in such a hurry to grow up! Auntie Cora can't take it!"

That made them giggle. Cheyenne, Evan's wife, stepped in and took the girls to get washed up for dinner, and then we all sat down around the table and dished up the delicious-smelling meal. I spooned some of the vegetable medley onto my plate first, then made sure Selene got a piece of chicken before she read me the riot act.

"Have you tried the chicken yet, Roger?" Mom asked.

"I'm just about to cut into it," he replied with a smile. He sliced into the roast chicken and placed a dollop in his mouth. His eyes fluttered closed, and he let out an appreciative groan. "Mmm. This is delicious, Lilac. I'm telling you, you should open a restaurant here in Winterspell. I'd be there every day!"

Mom laughed and waved her linen napkin at him. "Oh, stop. It's just a simple meal."

"It's really good, Mom," Evan agreed.

I nodded in agreement.

Selene was too busy stuffing her face to comment on the meal, although her remaining speechless truly was the highest compliment she could offer.

"So, Roger, tell us what you've been up to now that you're back in town," Mother said sweetly. "Did you get tired of the big city life?"

Roger finished chewing and washed down his mouthful of chicken with a sip of wine. "Well, I'll tell you what. Big city life isn't all it's cracked up to be."

"Oh, how so?"

"There's people all around you, yet you don't really know anybody. Everyone is always in such a hurry. Sure, there are things I liked about it. It was easy to get to live music performances and other big events that came to town, and it was nice to have an endless supply of restaurants and things, but for the most part it's actually kind of isolating to live in the city."

"Aww. It sounds like you might have just gotten a little homesick," Mom replied.

Roger smiled. "I'll say this: There's no place like home." He smiled at me, and for a moment, a lot of old feelings stirred up in my chest. I didn't want to feel those things, and a fresh wave of irritation toward my mom bubbled up.

"So, Cora," Evan said, trying to move past the awkwardness. "How are things going at Wicked Wicks? Every time Cheyenne and I drive past there, it looks like there's a lot of cars out front."

"It's been busy, that's for sure. Some days it seems like it's still the height of tourist season, but I'm sure things will calm down soon."

Mom's eyes glowed. "Are you still finding time to get out on the lake? You know, Roger and I were talking about kayaking yesterday. The two of you should plan a time to go together. I always worry about you going out on the water alone, Cora."

"I wear my life vest and I'm hardly a novice, Mother," I said through clenched teeth.

"We actually did kind of go on a little float together a couple of weeks ago," Roger said cheerfully.

Mom perked up in her seat while I cursed him silently in my head.

The agonizing dinner wore on and on, until the dessert course when I finally managed to drag Roger away while my mother checked on the firmness of the key lime pie.

I practically dragged him out onto the front porch and confronted him. "What do you think you're doing in there?" I demanded.

Roger frowned in confusion. "I'm not doing anything."

"Yes, you are. What's with all the 'oh, there's no place like home' stuff? Or talking about our kayak trip—it wasn't even a trip. We just happened to be out on the water at the same time and paddled near one another."

"Cora, why are you getting so upset about this? Clearly, accepting your mother's invitation was a mistake on my part, but I didn't want to be rude when she asked me over. I honestly didn't think you'd have a problem with it."

I rubbed my temples, my eyes closing for a moment.

"If you want, I can leave now," he offered.

My eyes popped open again. "No! Then I'll hear about it for the rest of the night, how I *scared* you off." I glanced over my shoulder, through the front window. Mom was carrying the pie into the dining room. "Come on," I said. "Let's just finish this thing."

I didn't wait for him to agree before I slipped back inside the house.

I spent the dessert course in silence, digesting

more than just the meal. I remained conflicted about my feelings for Roger. Every time I saw him, I grew more confused. I was happy with Clint, but still, something about seeing Roger, about sitting around my family's table like old times, it muddied the waters and left me reeling. If I was truly over him, why did it matter at all? And more pressing, would I always feel this way? Or would it one day just fade completely away?

Roger left shortly after pie, making an excuse about a work thing in the morning. A few minutes after he left, Evan and Cheyenne packed up the sugar-high twins to get home for bath time. That left me to help my mother clean up and pack away leftovers. I tried to avoid discussing Roger at all. I truly didn't want to get locked into another argument.

So, I turned the topic to Aunt Lavender. Selene and I took turns laying out our progress over the past week, including the details about Salvatore Greco's mysterious death and the possibility that Lavender had a potentially dangerous book in her possession prior to her abduction.

Mom shook her head. "What would your aunt be doing with such a thing?"

"From what I understand, she sort of borrowed it accidentally on purpose and forgot to return it—

maybe. Anyway, I thought I'd ask if she'd mentioned anything about it, or if you had any idea where she might have stashed it. Like, maybe she has a safety deposit box or something?"

"No, I can't say that I do. As for the deposit box, if she had one, she never mentioned it to me." Mom frowned as she hand-dried a plate.

We talked a little more about Lavender, all of us shadowboxing around the fact we were worried sick about her. I took my leftovers and drove home, while Selene reenacted the more painfully awkward moments from the dinner.

She didn't stop until I threatened to switch her to Walmart brand cat food. Of course, Selene's teasing was nothing compared to the torment offered up by my own mind.

I was going to have to figure out how I felt about Roger, and soon.

13

*A*fter the high-stress dinner at my mom's house, I took a few "me" days, where I reverted to my pre-Selene routine of going to work, then going to the lake until sunset, before getting takeout and returning home for some reading or mindless TV. I'd hit dead ends on all fronts. I had no idea where Lavender was or how to find her. I'd emailed August Nell's office to see about getting a meeting, but so far hadn't found a way past the gate-keepers who managed his inbox. My mom had texted a few times since Tuesday, but I'd kept my responses brief. I didn't want there to be tension between us, but I also wanted to set a boundary. As for Clint, he was busy with a big work thing and somewhat unavailable, which was fine with me. I needed some time and space after the whole scene with Roger.

By Saturday, I was starting to come out of my funk, which was a good thing because I needed to be on my A-game for the weekend rush at Wicked Wicks. Selene was suspiciously absent most of the day, and by the time I was getting ready to close, I was wondering just what she'd done with herself all day. While I'd been self-soothing with cookie dough ice cream and long evenings on the lake, she'd been off doing her own investigative work.

When I stepped out of the shop to lock up, I checked my watch. There was still time to swing by the library. It was sprinkling out, and while I wasn't opposed to kayaking in the rain, the idea of a cozy night in with some new books sounded more appealing.

So I biked over to the library, locked my bike up outside, and hurried toward the front door, pausing only to shake the water from my lightweight jacket underneath the awning before going inside. The library was warm and quiet, and the smell of books beckoned me deeper inside. I spotted Frankie at the main check-out desk and scurried past, hoping she wouldn't notice me.

"Cora?" a loud voice called.

Cringing, I spun toward it and found Selene waltzing down one of the aisles. I peeked over my shoulder, and sure enough, the cat's greeting had attracted Frankie's attention. She pursed her lips and quickly turned away to tend to the next person in line.

"Selene? What are you doing here?" I asked, turning back to the cat.

"Looking for information about Obin's book," she said. "Isn't that what you're doing here? You finally decided to stop wallowing and make yourself useful?"

Before I could defend myself, she wheeled around the end cap display and sauntered down the next aisle. "I decided we needed a new angle," she continued, not bothering to look back and check whether or not I was following along.

Muttering to myself, I jogged two paces to catch up with her. "A new angle, huh?"

"Sal wasn't the first person to get his mitts on Obin's book," Selene replied. "That book has launched dozens, maybe even hundreds, of treasure hunting campaigns. And there have been plenty of books, articles, even a documentary series, about Obin's quests."

"Okay." I nodded. "So, you think that even without the book we might be able to figure out what kind of quest Aunt Lavender was gearing up for?"

"We'll get to know the players," Selene said. "Lavender must have approached people as a part of her research. If she let it slip that she had the book itself, well, that news would have spread quickly through the treasure-hunting circle. If we can figure out those names and faces, we'll have a new pool of possible suspects to look into."

I had to hand it to her, it made sense. The majority of magical beings and creatures couldn't care less about a musty old book, even if it was said to contain some kind of treasure map. It was almost funny how mundane and normal the lives of witches, wizards, mages, and fairies could be. Non-magic humans would likely assume that every day in Winterspell played out like something from a fantasy movie, when in reality, magic or not, most creatures craved routine and the comfort of the familiar. Not everyone wanted to go off on some life-altering quest, or battle dragons just to find out if they had a pile of gold.

"Come on," Selene said, leading me to a table full of books, "I'll show you what I've found so far."

A passing librarian stopped to politely ask if Selene needed any more assistance. "I'm good. My apprentice is here now," the cat told her.

"Apprentice?" I frowned. "Hardly."

Selene jumped onto the table and padded over to an open book, its pages pinned down by a paperweight in either corner. Clearly, she'd had the poor librarian at her beck and call for the past however long she'd been in here. "Listen up, you might learn a thing or two," she told me. "Have you heard of Tabitha Hardwick?"

I shook my head as I pulled out a chair and sat down. "No, can't say that I have. Who is she?"

"This is her memoir," Selene said, gesturing with a paw. "She's essentially a magical Indiana Jones with a travel vlog."

"Oh?"

"She personally saw and handled the Obin tome at one point or another. There's another one over there, written by a fire mage who ran an expedition to find a sunken pirate ship that had a chest of gold."

"How was that related to magic?"

"Apparently, the ship is guarded by undead pirates. No one who went after it ever came back, until this guy."

"Yikes. Okay. So, all of these books are somehow connected to Obin's book?"

Selene nodded. "Yes, and you're going to check them all out."

"Right." I got to my feet and began gathering everything up. I was going to bump up against my limit on total number of check-outs allowed, but generally the Winterspell librarians weren't too persnickety about such things.

Of course, no sooner had I thought that than I remembered who was currently manning the check-out desk.

"Oh boy," I muttered, getting in line behind a family. "Maybe we should go to the one upstairs," I whispered to Selene.

Selene eyed me. "You want to carry all of those upstairs?"

My arms were full to bursting, and it seemed the cat had a talent for choosing the heaviest books in the library to take home.

"No," I said after a moment.

"Didn't think so."

The family ahead of us took a few minutes, as each of the three small children picked out a special toy from a basket. I smiled as I watched them. I remembered back to my own childhood when I participated in the library's read-a-thon program. For every book read, a child was awarded a certain number of points, and eventually could save up enough to cash out for a prize.

Once the kiddos had made their selections, the parents shepherded them along, and I started to take a step forward—only to be cut off by a polished-looking man in a tailored suit.

"Yo! Back of the line, Mister!" Selene exclaimed.

The man didn't so much as flinch. He spread his palms along the counter and leaned in toward Frankie. "I'd like to see the books donated by the Greco estate."

Frankie blinked. "Um, there have been a number of tomes donated posthumously by the late Mr. Salvatore Greco—"

"Great, that's great. So, uh, how much for the lot?"

The man reached into his pocket and withdrew a leather wallet.

"I'm sorry?" Frankie's brow furrowed. "I'm not sure I understand—"

The man flashed a smile, but his jawline tightened. "I'm buying all of the Greco books, *please*. Name your price."

Frankie was starting to look a little flustered.

"Sir, the books are not for sale. They were donated to the library. Once they have been processed and enter into our system, you'll be able to check them out."

"No." The man shook his head as he dug into his wallet and produced a thick stack of green bills. "No, that won't work. I want to take the books tonight. We can do this all under the table if that makes it easier. I'll make it worth your while."

A pinch of anger crept into Frankie's eyes, making them a little harder. "I am the head librarian of this establishment, *sir*. You cannot bribe me or any of my staff to sell books intended for this library. Salvatore's will was very specific. And even if I wanted to go along with this … proposal, I wouldn't be able to. The books are not here yet. All I have is a list of what we can expect to receive when the time comes."

The man straightened up, giving me my first good look at him. Tall and thin, almost lanky. Everything about him screamed wealth, even setting aside the fistful of—were those *hundreds?*

Jeepers.

His lean face drew back in a smile, though it looked faker than the extended warranty telemarketers kept trying to sell me.

"I'm sorry, perhaps I'm not making myself clear. My name is August Nell." He paused, as if that alone would bowl Frankie over.

She didn't react, but my heart certainly did. It jumped into my throat as I looked down at Selene, ensuring she'd heard it, too.

"Well, it's nice to meet you. We always appreciate fellow book lovers around here, but as to the matter of Mr. Greco's books, I'm afraid I have nothing left to say on the matter," Frankie said. Her tone seemed as strained as her smile.

August Nell's jaw tightened. "I see. That's unfortunate."

He turned and stalked away from the counter, making a beeline for the doors.

"Should we go after him?" I asked Selene.

Frankie's voice interrupted before I could make a decision, "Ugh, not you again. Come to accuse me of another crime, have you? Why can't you leave me alone?"

"No, no, no," I said, lumbering forward to relieve my arms of the large stack of books. "Stars, that burns," I complained as I shook out my arms and wiggled my fingers. "Frankie, I swear, I'm not here to accuse you of anything this time. It all really was just a misunderstanding, I think."

Frankie's eyes widened. "You *think?*"

"Well, it's just—"

"The little twerp next door busted your alibi," Selene interjected. "Said he saw you sneaking out around midnight while he was in the middle of his nerdfest of a video game."

Frankie shook her head in slack-jawed disbelief. "What is wrong with you? Do you just wander through life always assuming the worst of people? I told you, yes, I was angry at Salvatore, but I never— and I mean *never*, considered acting on those frustrations, other than—well, other than yelling at Ernesto at Merlin's Well, but that was a mistake and I have since apologized to him."

Frankie huffed an exasperated sigh. "If Chris saw me leaving my house, it was when I went to the corner store for a sleeve of Oreos and a cheap bottle of wine, all right? There! That's my big secret. You caught me. I had a terrible night, and I went out to get a little comfort. I was back home ten minutes later, and if you don't believe me, you can ask Orlando. He works the late shift, and he knows me."

"I really am sorry, Frankie. I swear, I wouldn't be pushing this hard, but it's—" I paused and exhaled slowly. "My aunt Lavender was kidnapped. The police aren't taking it seriously, so I'm left on my own—"

"Hey, what am I? Chopped liver?" Selene piped in.

"Selene was my aunt's familiar, and we're both worried sick, and probably not thinking clearly."

"Speak for yourself," Selene interjected. "My mind is as sharp as razor wire!"

I rolled my eyes.

Frankie's expression softened somewhat. "I—I didn't know. I'm sorry about your aunt. She's a special lady."

"Thank you." I swallowed the unexpected ball of emotion in my throat. Outside of the police, Clint, and my own family, this was the first time I was really talking about Aunt Lavender with someone. "Sal called and left a message on her machine a few days ago. He didn't know she was missing, and he was railing about this book he thought she'd swiped from him—anyway, long story short, we think figuring out what happened to him might somehow help us figure out what's happened to her."

Frankie nodded.

"It's not an excuse though, you're right. I've been completely out of line here, and I truly am sorry."

She didn't respond right away, instead opting to

begin scanning in the books piled between us. When she flipped over the third one, she glanced up at me. "Any chance Salvatore's missing book was the *Odyssey of Obin Amorath*?" she asked.

"Yes! You know it?"

"Well, I mean, any librarian worth their salt *knows* about the book. But I've never seen it before." She squinted. "Wait, so you're saying Salvatore had it?"

I shrugged. "That's what he told us, the day before he died, actually."

"Wow." Frankie clucked her tongue and finished scanning in the books. "Well, it looks like you've got a good primer here on all things Obin Amorath. If there's anything I can do to help, let me know, okay? If I can help Lavender, I will."

"Thanks, Frankie. That really means a lot to me."

We headed out of the library a few moments later, my arms once again begging for mercy under the weight of Selene's research pile. "You're going to have to hoof it," I told her as I deposited the books into the basket.

"I don't have hooves," she complained. "Just let me ride on your shoulder."

"No! You always scratch the bejeebus out of me."

"I'll be delicate, you little doily."

I swung my leg over the bike. "Nope. It's either the purse or you walk."

"The purse?" Selene whined. "But I don't want to be like one of those yappy little ankle biters."

"Suck it up, buttercup."

Selene shot me a cold glare, but then acquiesced to being loaded into my crossbody purse for the ride home.

"I say we officially cross Frankie off the list," I said as we started down the road. "My gut tells me she's being honest. If we want to double-check with the mini-mart guy, we can, but I'm not sure I see the need."

"What about August Nell?" Selene asked.

"He was a piece of work, wasn't he?"

"He was a piece of something," Selene muttered.

"Maybe we should have gone after him, I don't know. I've emailed his office, but no one has given me more than a canned response about the message being forwarded on and thanking me for my patience."

I chewed my lip for a moment, then continued my stream of thoughts. "He wants Sal's books. Badly. And I get the feeling he isn't going to take Frankie's no as a final answer."

Selene's ears went back. "You can tell a lot about

a person based on first impressions. I'm telling you, this guy is bad news."

If August Nell was our killer, then that would make him very dangerous indeed. Anyone callous enough to kill over a book would surely kill again to keep that murder under wraps.

I resolved to find as much out about August Nell as I could. And soon.

14

"This is the place?"

The four-story square office building was painted a bland gray color. A series of cement planters filled with some variety of a variegated shrub were the only things bringing any color to the exterior. It didn't look fit for a millionaire, but then Winterspell is a tad short on skyscrapers with helipads on the rooftops.

"That's the address from the flyer," Selene said, flicking her tail at the black numbers mounted in the stone facade above a set of glass doors.

Technically speaking, August Nell was based out of San Francisco, but during our research phase, we'd learned that he had properties all up and down the West Coast, most of which weren't even in magical communities like Winterspell. I had no idea why he kept an office in Winterspell of all places. With his wealth and connections, he could have a second office in any number of exciting locales.

Somehow in the process of emailing August Nell's office, my email address had been stuck into an automated newsletter targeting aspiring developers. As it turned out, August was hosting a conference for magical real estate agents, developers, and flippers, right here in Winterspell at his so-called "home away from home"—the Winterspell Chalet. The conference wasn't for another three months— and came with an eye-watering admission cost. I'd slid down to the bottom to unsubscribe myself when I spotted an address in teeny tiny print, and realized it was a business address I hadn't seen on his main website.

"You ready for this?" I asked Selene.

"I was born ready," she assured me.

"Which time?" I teased. "You always say you're on your ninth life."

"That's because I am. Yeesh. I'm surprised your mother was able to birth you, what with that thick skull of yours."

The glass doors slid open, and we stepped into a comfortably appointed lobby. A water feature hissed nearby, burbling into a little pool where bamboo grew. Or at least I thought it was bamboo. The thick carpet absorbed the sound of my footfalls as I approached the front reception desk. It appeared August rented out the entire building, as it was his name affixed to the wall behind the desk in a bold serif font.

It was a busy Monday morning, and it seemed as though everyone was running late for something.

"Hello," I said, smiling at the receptionist. "I'd like to—"

"That's hardly my concern." Her eyes narrowed, and her voice dropped to a low growl. I looked to Selene to see what I had done wrong, but my familiar seemed just as confused as I was. "You know that Mr. Nell expects a high degree of attention to detail. Not only were we sent the wrong flowers, but we were also shorted an arrangement. So, no, I don't care that purple day lilies are hard to come by right now, just make it happen!"

The woman sighed and tapped a button, then turned her gaze and a smile my way. "I'm so sorry you had to hear that. How can I assist you?"

I blinked. "I'm here to see August Nell, if that's possible."

The woman's smile froze, and her eyes seemed almost … afraid. "Do you have an appointment? I didn't see anything on his calendar for this morning." The woman's gaze drifted to the right, consulting a large computer screen.

"I don't have an appointment, but—"

"I'm sorry, but without an appointment, there is nothing I can do. Mr. Nell is a very busy man." The receptionist pointedly folded her hands on top of the desk and smiled sweetly. "Tell you what, I can take a message and if he has time, he will get in touch with you at his convenience. I'm sure you can understand. Time is money, after all."

"Could you tell him it's regarding Salvatore Greco? I really think he will be interested in what I have to say. He and Mr. Greco were acquaintances. If I could just speak with him for a few moments, I won't have to take up any more of his time than that."

She sniffed derisively and plucked a business card from a holder on the desk. As she extended it toward me, she tapped an acrylic nail against the glossy cardstock. "There's an email address here. I'm sure someone on his executive team can forward on your information."

"I've already tried that. I got a canned response and put on some kind of real estate marketing email list."

"Well, as Mr. Nell always says, persistence is 99% of the secret recipe to success!"

Selene jumped up onto the counter and peered at the woman, then looked up at me. "She's kidding, right?"

The receptionist recoiled slightly, her rolling chair scooting back from the desk a few inches.

Selene leaned in. "She's stonewalling us, Cora. How are we going to get past her and talk to August Nell when he's got the Terminator as his recep-tionist?"

My eyes narrowed to slits. I had a plan, but it was pretty evil.

"Selene," I said. "Do you remember that song you were singing to me the other day?"

"Oh, you mean 'There's no food in my bowl'?"

"Yes, that one."

"What about it?"

"I think you should sing it. As loudly as possible."

"What?" Her ears went back in suspicion. "But

you hate my singing in general, and that song in particular."

"Yes, and so will everyone else." She caught the wicked gleam in my eye and grinned.

"Now you're speaking my language. Ahem. Mi mi mi mi … do re mi fa so la ti doooo … Lion Face. Lemon Face. Lion Face. Lemon Face—"

"Get on with it!"

Selene gave me one final glare before belting out a rendition of her song. "Oh, there's no food in my boooooowl, the humans are stupid for suuuuuure. They open their mouths and I see manuuure…"

All around us in the lobby, the hard-working urban professionals clasped their hands over their ears and groaned, their faces masks of misery. The receptionist looked on with the kind of horror usually reserved for gas station bathrooms on Taco Tuesdays. "Please, make it stop doing that!"

"I don't have the power to make it stop. Only you have the power to make it stop."

The woman glared at me, but after a quick look around at all the attention we were receiving, she quickly surrendered. She got on her little Bluetooth headset and made the arrangements. Selene sang the entire time, much to everyone's chagrin—even my own. It was turning into a bit of a Frankenstein's monster situation. Luckily, I'd built up a hefty toler-ance to Selene at that point. All those poor office workers and the sassy receptionist didn't stand a chance.

They were defeated the moment Selene started singing.

"Mr. Nell will see you in his office now," the receptionist hollered above Selene's god-awful screeching. I swear it was peeling the paint and making the lights flicker, it was so bad. "Please make her shut up."

"Selene," I said, touching the cat on her back. "Selene, you can stop now."

"But I'm just working my way up to the hook."

"Yes, I know, that's why I'm in a hurry to stop you. Besides, we won. We got our audience with August Nell."

"I guess my performance was so awesome that everyone couldn't take the beauty. Like beholding the true face of Zeus and exploding into dust because you can't handle it."

"Yes, I'm sure that's exactly what happened. It's the likeliest of scenarios."

Augustʼs office was on the top floor, and while the building was only four levels, it still provided a beautiful panoramic view of Winterspell, with every wall of the office but one being made of glass.

A different receptionist gave us a dirty look as she ushered us into the office where August sat behind a long, low modern desk. He rose at our entrance, adjusting his tie and plastering that phony smile of his across his face.

"Well, as a businessman I've had my fair share of people behaving strangely to gain an audience. You, however, are the first one to serenade my entire workforce with the dulcet tones of a feline familiar."

"Did you hear that? I have dulcet tones."

"Only to deaf people." I looked up to August Nell's implacable smile and tried to do the same. "Mr. Nell, thank you for taking the time to see us. I promise I'll make this quick."

August gestured at the chairs opposite him and then retook his seat. I perched on the edge of the cushy seat, eager to get to business. "My name is Cora Hearth, and this is Selene. We were at the library the other day and overheard you speaking with the head librarian about some rare books. More specifically, Salvatore Greco's collection."

August's expression changed. He clearly hadn't expected that. Perhaps he thought I'd come to pitch him on some investment opportunity or to ask for personalized advice on how best to diversify my portfolio, or whatever he got into.

"Salvatore? I see. Yes, it's such a tragedy." He pushed his glasses up higher on his nose, the mechanical movement somehow reminding me of a praying mantis. "He will be missed by many. Myself included."

"How exactly did the two of you know each other?"

August smiled. "I do a lot of business with a lot of different people in a lot of different places, Miss Hearth."

"Yes, but you specifically purchased rare tomes of magic and literature from Salvatore Greco, didn't you?"

His lips may have twitched, but it was hard to tell. His gaze never wavered. "I'm sorry, I must have missed your connection to all of this. Are you a family member? Or ..." He let his voice trail off, leaving room for me to fill in the gaps.

"I know Salvatore had the *Odyssey of Obin Amorath*," I said bluntly. I'd worry about whether the admission was a mistake later.

As it was, the bait worked. August's demeanor changed as he leaned forward and braced his forearms on the edge of his desk, peering at me with deepened interest. "So, he *did* have it? I was beginning to think he'd been pulling my leg. Tell me, where is the book now?"

"You were going to buy it from him, then?" I asked.

"I offered Sal quite a generous sum for the tome, yes. He told me he needed to think about my offer, which I took to mean he had a few other collectors on the line, so I upped my bid."

"But that didn't work?"

"No, he kept stalling. In fact, during our last conversation, he took an almost hostile tone with me. I was most disappointed."

"Disappointed enough to kill the old geezer?" Selene blurted.

"Selene!" I gasped.

August laughed. "You honestly think I would risk my empire over a dusty old book?" He shook his head, his grin widening. "No. It would have been an impressive trophy, but not worth killing for."

"And we're supposed to just believe you?" Selene asked.

I cringed. This was the Frankie situation all over again, except I was pretty sure the guy on the other side of the table could do a lot more than send my library card through the shredder if he wanted to punish me for crossing him.

"So, you can sing, and you're a detective? Is that right?" August asked Selene. "Fascinating."

He shifted his gaze back to me. "You know, I like to collect all kinds of things. Is your pet available for sale?"

I blinked. "I—I'm sorry, but *what?*"

Selene hissed.

August laughed and leaned back in his chair. "I jest. You two are clearly quite bonded."

"Like Gorilla Glue," I muttered.

"As to your question, I was at a charity event the night Salvatore passed into the Stardust. If you'd like to verify it, you can find roughly a hundred witnesses here in Winterspell, as it was hosted at my hotel. Perhaps you've been, the Winterspell Chalet?"

Selene scoffed. "This one makes candles for a living, we're lucky we get extended cable. There's definitely no dimes in the budget for a nice massage at that day spa, unless you can get us a discount? Some kind of voucher?"

August's eyes gleamed. "I admire the hustle. Tell you what, for your trouble and excellent entertainment value, I'll see to it my assistant sends you home with a gift certificate, to show there are no hard feelings."

"That's really unnecessary," I stammered.

August rose and pressed a button on his desk phone. As soon as I got to my own feet, the door swung open and the sour-faced assistant returned to ferry us out again.

I glanced over my shoulder. "Thank you for your time, Mr. Nell."

"Can you believe that chump had the nerve to give us these?" Selene groused in the car. Between us on the console sat a pair of paper gift certificates, and the paper they were printed on likely cost more than the certificates themselves: $5 each. Which the Icefire Day Spa, tucked inside the luxe Winterspell Chalet, wasn't enough to even get one toe painted.

"We did kind of have it coming," I said. "We made a ruckus in his lobby and then you flat-out accused him of being a murderer. You've got to stop that, by the way. I go out of my way to naturally extract information and then you charge in. It's like swinging a wrecking ball when you meant to use a scalpel."

"Well, that guy's a ghoul either way," Selene muttered as I turned over the engine of my car. The radio kicked on softly, playing a country ballad. I cracked the front windows to get a cross breeze going. It was mild outside, but the interior of the car still felt a little stuffy after being parked in the sun.

"Just because we don't like him doesn't mean he's a killer. His alibi is pretty solid."

Selene fell silent. "I still don't like him."

"I know the feeling, but we have to be objective about this investigation, Selene. Not liking the guy isn't an indictment. We need solid evidence to connect him to the murder of Salvatore Greco. It's that simple."

"Well, let's not race to conclusions just yet. Maybe he was lying about the charity shindig!"

I doubted it, but I decided to humor her. I got the phone out of my purse and pulled up the social media page of the Chalet. Scanning back a week, it was easy to spot the event, and the date matched up.

"There's hundreds of pictures here," I told the cat as I scanned through, occasionally flipping my phone around to show her one. "It would take all afternoon to go through it all, but I see August in several of them. Safe to say his story checks out, and we can check him off our list."

"I think we should check the time stamps," Selene said with an air of stubbornness. "But not on that thing. It hurts my eyes. We need the bigger screen of your laptop."

Sighing, I pulled out onto the road and headed for home. "Okay, but we don't have all day. I need to get the shop opened."

"Why bother? That place is a ghost town on Monday mornings. It's worse than that, actually. At least if you had ghosts there'd be someone to talk to!"

"Believe me, Selene, you provide all the commentary I could ever need."

We drove home and fired up the laptop. As soon as it came on, Selene groaned at the update in progress screen. "Oh, man, come on, installing update 13 of 567? Do you ever even turn this thing on, Cora?"

"It usually just lets me skip past it," I answered with a shrug.

After I spent a solid ten minutes watching a loading bar inch across the screen—and then do so again—my laptop was finally awake and ready to use. I logged in and went back to the Winterspell Chalet's social page. The cover photo at the top read *35th Annual Charity Gala* and featured a photo of August Nell, his arms around two of the other donors.

"Pay attention to the time stamps of when they were posted," Selene snapped. "He could have ducked out at some point."

"Salvatore's house is a good twenty-five-minute drive from the Chalet. He would have had to be gone for at least an hour, from his *own* event. Not likely. Besides, just because someone posts a photo at a certain time doesn't mean it was taken then."

"Darn technology, what is it really good for?" Selene grumbled as I scrolled through the photos. August Nell showed up in the background of several and was the subject of a photo all his own.

"So, Miss Smarty Pants, how do we tell what time these photos were taken?"

I squinted at the screen. "Well, judging by the

depleted level of punch in the bowl behind August there, I'd say at least a few hours into the event."

Selene pawed the screen. "Next slide!"

"Careful, it's a touch screen and your toe beans are recognized as fingers."

The cat flashed her dainty fangs. "I know, how do you think you ended up with the complete series of *The Beverly Hillbillies* on Blu-ray?"

I groaned. "I *knew* that was you. It cost me twenty dollars to ship that stuff back for a refund. I don't even own a Blu-ray player."

"I know, that's what made it so funny." Selene stared at the screen.

"Anyway, we're sort of getting off topic here. Let's look at some of the other social media pages."

We found August Nell's picture showing up in several different feeds, along with a woman I assumed to be his wife or fiancée judging by their body language and the honking diamond ring on her hand.

"Satisfied yet?" I asked. "See what I mean about bias? We don't like him, but we still needed to look at the evidence before forming any kind of theory incriminating the guy."

"Yeah, yeah, enough with the I told you so's," Selene groused.

I scoffed. "Selene, you *love* saying I told you so."

"Yes, I know I love saying it. You want to know *why* I love saying it?"

I grimaced. "No, but I'm afraid you're going to tell me anyway."

"Right you are, bucko. I love saying it because it drives people crazy!"

"So, you can dish it out, but you can't take it?"

"I'm punching up. You hairless apes are running the world, like it or not, so anything I do or say is punching up. You, on the other hand, are the privileged opposable thumb–possessing species, so you'd be punching down. So don't punch down and say I told you so."

I rolled my eyes to the ceiling. "All right, fine. I need to get going anyway."

"Wait, check it out." Selene touched the screen with her paw, making the image jump. "Isn't that Michelle, Ernesto's wife?"

"It sure looks like her. Wow, she cleans up well. "It looks like she's speaking with August." I shook my head. "They seem pretty friendly."

"It looks like a candid shot. They didn't know their picture was being taken."

"I think you're right." I set the laptop aside. "This must be where they were talking about the book.

Remember, Michelle is the one who first brought August to our attention."

"So, Ernesto was out getting blasted while his wife was all dolled up and getting chatty with August Nell. Hmm. It's a small world."

I pointed a finger at her. "If you start singing that song, I swear to the Mother I'll evict your furry little butt so fast it'll make your head spin."

Grinning, Selene sat back on her haunches and started cleaning her paw. "Well, I wasn't *going* to, but thanks for the future ammo."

"Ugh!" I shoved off the couch, tossing my hands into the air.

15

As irritating as it was to admit, Selene was right about one thing, Wicked Wicks was turning into a ghost town on Mondays. I wound up finishing my custom orders, taking inventory, and getting a jump on restocking, with only a handful of customers sprinkled in between. I wound up closing early for the night and heading down to the lake.

The sky was a cotton candy swirl of pinks and purples as the sun made her exit. There was still at least another hour or so before dusk would fall, leaving me plenty of time for a walk around the trails surrounding the lake. I climbed over a fallen log that had been there since I was a child and picked my way carefully down to my secret beach. It wasn't really a secret, but most people stayed on the trail, so I rarely had to share my special little spot where I could sit and listen to the water lapping against the shore.

I picked my way through the copse of pines and gasped when I saw that someone was already there on my patch of beach.

Roger.

I started to turn around and flee, but then my weight finally strained a twig past the breaking point. He turned at the resulting audible snap and blinked.

"Cora?"

"Hi, Roger," I said with a deep, heavy sigh.

"What are you doing here?"

"Same as you, I imagine. Looking for a quiet place to think."

"I'm sorry," he said, getting up. "I was just about to leave, anyway."

"It's fine, Roger. Don't go on my account. We're adults. We can share." I offered a smile as a token of my sincerity.

He returned it, but there was a hesitancy in his eyes. "I wouldn't even know about this place if it weren't for you."

Heat burned my cheeks as my memory conjured a montage of steamy moments we'd shared right here, hidden away from the world. "I guess that's true."

"I feel lost, Cora."

My breath hitched in my throat at the hollowness of his voice. Scrambling over the last few branches and shrubs, I approached him and sank down to sit in the sand beside him. "What's going on? The other night at dinner you seemed so happy to be back again."

He exhaled a dry laugh. "Well, what was I supposed to say? That I'm a mess? That I'm living in a hotel because I can't figure out whether I should stay or go? I'm about to turn thirty-nine, Cora. Not all that far off from forty, and yet it feels like I'm a stupid, indecisive teenager all over again."

I stared down at my hands. "I'm really sorry. I had no idea."

"I should have never left. Not this place. Not my job here. Not … you."

My heart sank even lower as I brought my eyes to his. "Don't say that, Rodge. You went out, you took a chance. And yeah, it didn't work out, but if you'd stayed here, all you would have done is walked around wondering 'what if.' That's no way to live, either."

Roger leaned his head back against the large

boulder behind him and exhaled slowly, staring out at the lake through half-lidded eyes. "You're probably right." He chuckled. "You usually are. What's that like, anyway?"

I smiled. "I don't know if I agree with that. I've made *plenty* of mistakes. The latest one weighs in at about ten pounds and could eat me out of house and home in a week flat if I let her. Plus, you wouldn't believe the mess she leaves all over the house!"

Roger laughed. A real, genuine laugh, and something fluttered inside of me. Old memories rushed back, as though my skin had been soaked in them and now they were all evaporating and rushing to the surface.

When he rocked his head over to look at me, a smile still clung to his lips. "I missed you, Cora. Losing you is, and always will be, the biggest regret of my life."

"Roger, please—"

"I know," he interjected, holding up one hand. "I know. You've moved on, and I'm happy for you."

I quirked one brow and he laughed. "Okay, I'm working on being happy for you," he teased.

His eyes filled with an earnest light. "I was unhappy, and I thought that moving away would solve everything. But looking back, I know I should have hung in there. I should have fixed things."

I sighed. "Roger, we both know it wasn't just about you wanting to move out of Winterspell. Even if that job offer hadn't come along, we probably still would have separated at some point. We were turning into two different people than when we first met."

He bobbed his head. "I know. I should have put on the brakes when we first started drifting apart and tried to bring us back together. For that, I'm truly sorry."

I couldn't look at him in that moment. I turned away and stared at the painted sky. "I'm sorry that you didn't fight harder for us, too."

Roger shifted uncomfortably. "Look, I don't say all this to try and screw things up with your new guy. I just …"

"You just what?" I prompted when his voice trailed off.

"I just can't help feeling a little bit jealous."

Tears pricked at the corners of my eyes, and it was all I could do to nod. Forcing down the swell of emotions, I wrapped my arms around my knees and drew them toward my chest. "I think—I think it's too late for that."

"I know." Roger gently draped an arm over my shoulders. I stiffened, but then relaxed into his side.

In that moment, we weren't just ex-lovers. We were old friends, helping each other through the heartbreak.

So I leaned my head against his shoulder, just like I used to do, and we sat in silence for a long time, staring out at the sunset.

I CAME HOME FAIRLY late and after dishing out a lecture about her late dinner, Selene shifted her attention to nosing about in my personal life. "So, did you hang out at Clint's mom's place? Does he live down in the basement? Did he show you his baseball cards and try to get to second base?"

"Selene, you have the strangest speculations. I'm not sure Clint's mother's lake house even has a basement, for one thing. For another, he hardly lives with his mother—he's just staying with her for now."

"Isn't that what I said?" Selene asked.

"Not even close. Clint is doing something noble, stepping up for his mom when she's going through a lot. You're trying to tarnish it, and I won't stand for that, Selene. You can say whatever you want to about me, mock my crow's feet or weight or whatever makes you feel like you have some control over your life, but don't pick on Clint."

There was a long stretch of silence, and I hoped that I had finally shamed the cat into closing her mouth for a while. Alas, I was wrong.

"I see. Given how defensive you are on Clint's behalf, I can only surmise that you were with him! Now, you didn't spend the night, but that doesn't necessarily rule out carnality—"

"Selene!"

"I mean, particularly if old Clint has a few, ahem, shortcomings."

"What are you even going on about now?"

"You know, I'm too polite to say it bluntly, but if the wool's not worth the carding, then why stick around after the sheep is shorn if you catch my drift?"

I rolled my eyes. "That's revolting, on a couple different levels. And not that it's *any* of your business, but no. I wasn't with Clint. I went for a walk and then I bumped into Roger—"

As soon as the words left my mouth, I regretted them. Every consonant, every vowel, and every syllable. There was a moment where Selene's eyes went wide with a particularly wicked glow. Just as they had when a sparrow had flown into the window, bounced off, and landed prone right in front of her in Lavender's yard. That look of fresh, easy prey upon which to pounce ...

"You were with Roger? No freaking way! Ha! Wait until I tell Lilac."

"You can *not* tell my mom!"

Stars, what was I, back in middle school?

"Why not?" Selene asked. "She's going to get a kick out of it! She's been trying to get you guys back together since before the ink even dried on those divorce papers. She told me all about it the other night when we were over there, how much she hoped you two would just kiss and make up."

I scrubbed both hands over my face. Seriously, if this was some kind of nightmare, I wished someone would throw a bucket of ice water on me already.

"I don't want her interfering more than she already is," I snapped. "And you can get your mind out of the gutter. All we did was hang out for a little while. We didn't even do a lot of talking."

Selene snickered, and I slapped a hand over my face. "Okay, poor choice of words. That's not what I mean. I stumbled onto him by accident. He was at my private little beach—"

"Is that what they're calling it these days?" Selene interjected.

"Okay, that's it, I'm officially buying one of those super soaker water guns," I said, marching to find my laptop.

"Oh, come on, Cora. Lighten up! He was at the beach, and—"

I shifted a sidelong glance her way. "You swear you won't tell my mom?"

"Yeah, yeah, sure. What happened?"

"Nothing, like I said. We talked for a couple of minutes, and then we wound up just … sitting there for a while. It was nice. Reminded me of the way things used to be before we tried so hard to be husband and wife."

"Yeah, but that's how it starts. You seek out the familiar because it feels safe, but remember, Cora: he's your ex-husband for a reason. You get me? He's your ex for a reason. You should remember that. I can't have you turning into an emotional wreck, crying in the bathtub, gorging yourself on Häagen-Dazs, and forgetting to buy my food."

"Is that really all I'm good for?"

"Hmm. Well, that and you drive me to the store so I can buy scratchers."

"With *my* money," I interjected.

"I won a free ticket, by the way. That and any size slushie I want."

"A veritable dragon's hoard of treasure," I muttered. "I sure am glad we spent twenty dollars on scratchers so you could get a frozen drink and another scratcher card out of the deal."

"You say that now but wait until I trade this baby in and scratch off the big prize: Nine hundred thousand dollars, or nine hundred thousand glazed donuts."

I laughed. "Oh, come on now, Selene, you know that the nine hundred thousand donuts offer is just a gag. They don't seriously expect people to take almost a million donuts. How would they even ship them?"

"Exactly! That's the beauty of my plan. For the record, it would take approximately fifteen semi-tractor-trailers to haul and deliver that many donuts, which would also require refrigeration to keep them fresh. That must cost well over the nine-hundred-thousand-dollar prize, don't you think?"

"Erm, well, I don't know. That's an awful lot of money."

Selene barreled on. "So, I'll agree to settle out of court for an amount of money greater than the nine hundred thousand offered by the scratcher ticket, and they don't have to deal with the logistical nightmare of delivering almost a million glazed donuts. You feel me?"

"I feel that your greed and deviousness know no bounds." I laughed as I walked down the hall to my bedroom. "I also think you haven't read all of the fine print yet."

I DROVE into work that day since the skies were threatening rain. The clouds formed a stifling dome over the normally cool Winterspell, as the storm prepared to release its payload of precipitation.

By the time I parked in the alley behind my shop and opened for business, the clouds had broken free at last, spilling a deluge onto the city. Interestingly enough, my business picks up when it rains. I think people associate candles with coziness and warmth, so they tend to stop by on an overcast day more than on a sunny one once the seasons change.

I busied myself at the counter, pouring myself into work so I wouldn't have to talk to Selene about the Roger situation or her bizarre lottery scratcher scheme. If I wasn't helping a customer or ringing up a purchase, I was crafting candles behind the counter. Since I was caught up on custom orders, I tried experimenting with a new variety of candle, meant to give the illusion of a night in Hawaii. Personally, I'd never been, but I knew how to use Google and found that having a clear image in my mind was enough to make it work most of the time.

Mid-morning, I took a phone call from my wax provider, an older witch with an apiary on the outskirts of Winterspell. We chatted for a time until I started getting busy again. It was a comfort, in a way, since there was no way I had time to worry about Roger or the case or anything else.

In the early afternoon, shortly after a miniature rush of customers had come and gone, I was lowering the wick into a mold when the bells over my door rang.

"Welcome to Wicked …" My voice trailed off when I saw who it was. My mom. I recognized her graying blonde bob above the shelving before she came fully into view.

I shot a warning glance at Selene. "Two words: super soaker."

The cat scowled as she tucked her front paws under her chest.

I could count on the fingers of one hand the number of times my mother had visited my shop since it had opened. She loved my work but knew that I liked to be left on my own, and she didn't want to interfere.

"Hello, Cora. Selene."

"Hi, Mom," I said, pouring wax into the mold that contained a pinch of Hawaiian sand and a few petals from a hibiscus flower. "What brings you by? Do you need something?"

"I know you're very busy. It's why I almost never bother you at work, but this can't wait." She looked back at the entrance. "Maybe you should close up for a bit."

My heart sank. She would never consider making such a request unless things were dire. My mind spat out a half dozen terrible thoughts in rapid-fire, most of them revolving around my aunt.

"Oh—okay," I said, nodding numbly as I walked out from behind the counter to put up my "back in twenty minutes" sign.

I returned to the counter, as if the physical

barrier could somehow impede the bad news my mother was there to deliver. "What's going on, Mom?"

"It's Lavender, Cora. I've been trying to reach her for weeks, ever since you discovered she's been—" Mom broke off, unable to bring herself to finish.

I nodded, feeling my heart catch in my throat.

"Well, last night, I finally got a reply with the scrying mirror."

My heart thudded hard in my chest as a surge of elation pulsed through me. Lavender was alive!

Selene leaped out of her cubby and landed on the counter. "Where is she?"

I noticed that my mother did not share our joy. Her lips remained tight, pulled into a somber frown.

"Mom, what's wrong? What are you not telling us?"

She heaved a sigh. "As you know, a scrying mirror is not generally a tool used to speak with the living, but Lavender and I have some sort of bond that enables us to speak using divination practices. We've done it since we were kids. I used to think of it like those tin cans tied together with string, only we could be miles from one another."

"Right, but if you heard her, surely that means she's still—still … alive. Right, Mom?"

She looked out the window as a car drove past the shop. "This time it was different. There was no presence or warmth on the other side, and I couldn't see Lavender. I could only hear her."

"What was she saying?"

Mom shook her head. "I couldn't make much of it out. It was like I was hearing her voice from far away, across a body of water or some other vast space. Her voice was so faint." Mom pressed her eyes closed, the wrinkles at the edges creasing as she grimaced at the memory. "She was saying that she'd never give it up. That it was too dangerous. That she'd—that she'd take it to her grave."

Selene's tail drooped. "Her grave?"

I blinked in confusion. "Never give it up? Never give *what* up?"

"I—I don't know." Mom's eyes flickered open again, revealing glossy pupils. "I'm sorry. I lost the connection after that."

I turned to Selene. "Do you think she was talking about the Amorath text?"

"It's entirely possible. I doubt they're after her secret bologna cake recipe."

I shuddered. "She's still making those?"

"Unfortunately, yes. I had to go outside when she was—but I digress." Selene turned to Cora. "You're sure it was Lavender's voice you heard, and not some kind of trick?"

"I'm positive it was Lavender," my mother said firmly. "One hundred percent, even if I couldn't actually speak with her."

I stroked my chin in thought. "Mom, aren't there spells that can interfere with scrying?"

"There are many ways to interfere with a scrying, dear." Mom sighed. "Go figure that witches and warlocks are a secretive bunch. As soon as the first scrying mirror was made, there were minds at work to circumvent and hide from them."

"Have you tried to use the scrying mirror since last night?" Selene asked.

My mother shook her head. "No, I haven't. It takes a lot of power and concentration. Last night I looked deeper and further than I had at any time before. My powers aren't what they used to be. I'm afraid I won't be able to try again right away."

"And we can't consult someone else, because as you said, scrying mirrors don't really work like that for other people," I added. "It has to be you."

Mom nodded, her expression turning more sorrowful.

I rounded the counter and pulled her into an embrace. Her shoulders shook as I held onto her.

"It's going to be okay, Mom. We're going to find her. We won't stop until we do."

Mom nodded but she continued to dab at her eyes when we pulled apart.

I offered a cautious smile. "Ultimately, this is good news, can't you see that?"

Selene flicked her tail. "How is it good news if Lilac couldn't even talk to Lavender?"

"Because it means that Aunt Lavender is still alive," I said, sniffling a little bit. "We're not too late."

"Don't get me started on that," Selene said, her voice wavering. "If you start crying, I'm going to cry. I just want to bring Lavender home, that's all. I know she's annoying as all get out, but I miss her. Right now, I'd eat a dozen bologna cakes if it meant getting her home, and that's saying something!"

"I'd join you," Mom said, smiling through the tears. "And you're right, they're ghastly."

We all laughed together, then Mom spoke again, "I know you're supposed to tell stories from the beginning, but let's just skip to the end of this one. Lavender is alive, and we're going to bring her home safe. The end."

I grabbed her hand. "We'll find her. I know we will."

16

*M*y mother hung around the shop until closing time. I think she didn't quite know what to do with herself and wanted to try and be helpful. Maybe she just needed a distraction. In any case, she helped me restock shelves and even sold a few candles to a customer, though she let me deal with the cash register. At closing time, she helped me tidy up while I broke down the till.

There was a kind of energy flowing through me, an enthusiasm I hadn't felt in some time. No one had come out and said it directly, but I think over the past couple of weeks, we'd all begun to silently wonder if our efforts to find Lavender hadn't changed into a mission to recover her body. With my mother's confirmation of Lavender's still-breathing status, we'd all drunk deep of the bittersweet nectar of hope. It lent a purpose to our movements, an extra spring in our step, and a bit more alertness to every detail.

Once I turned out the lights and locked the doors, I turned to my mother. "What's our next move?"

"We could try going over Lavender's place one more time," Selene offered. "Maybe Lilac could try the mirror again, using a different object."

I groaned in dismay, and my mother sighed and shook her head. "I'm afraid it's not the objects that are the problem. It's me. Maybe there is some kind of magical supercharger out there somewhere."

"What? Like a Red Bull for magic powers?" I asked.

Mom laughed, and it was good to see her smile. "Maybe!"

"Well, if it was at Lavender's, we would have found it by now. We've been over that place with a fine-tooth comb."

"Oh, I doubt that," Selene countered. "We've barely gotten started on the attic."

"Yeah, but judging by the layer of dust on everything up there, Lavender hasn't spent much time up there either."

"All right, then what do you suggest?" Selene asked. "We go home, nuke a TV dinner, and send out good vibes into the universe? Oh no, sorry, Aunt Lavender. I could have saved you but digging through your crap one more time was just too much effort. Yup, it was far more important that I caught up on *Love Island*—"

"All right, all right, we'll go back to Lavender's house," I said, throwing my hands up in the air. "For goodness's sake, Mom, why do you just stand there while Selene goes on these tirades?"

"What do you want me to do about it, kiddo?"

"I want you to, well, intervene."

She turned to look at Selene. "Bad kitty. Don't tease Cora."

"Thanks, Mom. That was *super* helpful."

We piled into my mom's car and drove over to Lavender's house. I was starting to dread the mere sight of the place. I knew that within dwelt dust bunnies waiting to tickle my nostrils. And the attic likely had a whole host of creepy crawlies who'd turned the maze into their own personal ecosystem.

I also knew, in spite of my many reservations, that we really didn't have much choice but to go and investigate Lavender's house one more time. Dust bunnies and all.

Mom got out of the car and rolled up her sleeves, ready to work.

"I've got to warn you, it's pretty bad in there," I told her.

Mom gave a rueful smile. "Oh, believe me. I've been dealing with your aunt and her pack rat tendencies for a lot longer than you."

"Pack rat? No, I think we're way past that," Selene said. "I'd say she's more like an absent-minded dragon who forgot they were supposed to collect treasure and began hoarding random crap instead."

I had to agree with the cat. I started to say so, when my muscles froze, then jerked, as though I'd accidentally touched a live wire or electric fence. As I was reeling from the jolt, my entire spinal column lit up with an icy cool blast and I shuddered before my legs turned to jelly and sent me flopping onto the grass.

"Cora, honey, are you all right?" Mom kneeled beside me in the grass and placed the back of her hand against my head.

"I think so," I said as the last of the shivers passed. "I don't know what happened."

"Do you need to go to the clinic? Come on, let me help you up."

With her help, I sat up and rubbed the back of my head. Another shiver coursed through me. "I—I don't know. I feel like there's something terribly wrong. Like some kind of premonition. A dark cloud."

My mother swiveled her gaze about, lights dancing in her hand as she prepared a magical defense. "I don't see anything."

"Not here," I said, massaging the bridge of my nose. "It seems to have come on with a headache, too. There's something wrong, but not here."

Selene crept over, her hackles raised.

A new rush of pain flooded through me and suddenly I saw a flash of an image in my mind. "Sal?"

"Sal?" Mom said.

"I'm seeing his house for some reason. It's so clear in my mind." I squeezed my eyes closed.

"Oh! The ward!" Selene exclaimed.

I popped one eye open. The pain and the vision were fading, but my nerves still felt on edge. "What?"

"Uhh ... well, you see, when we were at Sal's place, I may have kind of, sort of *used* you as a conduit to cast a teensy little security ward on his property."

"You *what*?" I sputtered. "I'm going to kill you!"

I lunged for the cat.

"Take it easy, Cora!" Mom said. "Selene, what kind of ward?"

"It's rigged to let us know if someone trespasses at Sal's. Someone crosses the threshold after a certain hour, and boom!" The cat got closer and peered up into my eyes as though she were checking me for signs of distress. "It's linked to your autonomic nervous system. You feel a 'fight or flight' response and it's linked to the spell."

"Okay, and how do we make it stop?" Mom asked.

"It's mostly over now," I told her. "I'm fine."

"Are you sure?"

I nodded and slowly got to my feet.

"Does the spell give you any indication of who might have breached the perimeter?" Mom asked Selene.

"No, it's not that refined. Now, if I'd had Cora's active participation, I might have been able to manage that, but—"

"You didn't even ask me!" I snapped. "Where do you get off just using me like a magic wand with legs? I didn't even know you could do that."

The possibilities were downright terrifying.

"Oh, yes, because you're so well known for being malleable to my suggestions," Selene sniffed.

"All I can say is that you'd better not have given me a splitting headache over a hungry raccoon or rat or something."

"No, I set it to only go off for bipedal creatures. Give me some credit, Cora."

"What if it's a witch shifted into a four-legged form?"

Selene frowned. "You know, that's actually a good point. I didn't think of that. Oh well, hindsight is always twenty-twenty. We'll workshop it."

"So, should we go to Salvatore's house and see who it is?" Mom asked. "I mean, for all we know it's just his lawyer or a housekeeper."

Heaving a sigh, I headed back to Mom's car. "Our best bet is to go over and take a look for ourselves."

We got into the car and before I buckled my seatbelt, Mom reached across and opened the glove box. A black cylinder was tucked inside. "Mom? Is that bear spray?"

She nodded. "If it turns out to be nothing, then fine. But if not … best be prepared for anything."

I glared at Selene as we drove toward Salvatore's estate. "This isn't over, Selene. Not by a long shot."

"We're not talking about it; I'm not thinking about it," Selene said, curling up for a nap on the seat beside me. "Kinda seems to me like it's over."

17

*M*y sense of urgency and alarm slowly dissipated, and once we turned onto the private drive for Salvatore's place, it was like a smothering blanket fell over the smoldering flames of my fight or flight reflex. I sighed in relief and leaned back in my seat, finally able to have clear thoughts again.

Mom pulled the car over to the side of the private lane when we were still a good distance from the manor house. "So, should we all go?"

"We could send Selene to look around," I suggested, casting a glance over my shoulder into the back seat. "But if something goes down, she can't call for help."

"Oh, yes. I'm such a damsel in distress," Selene muttered.

"We'll all go," I said, already opening the passenger door.

Mom and Selene climbed out after me. "All right, we're going in stealthy, but there's a problem: his landscape design doesn't give us much cover to work with while approaching the house," I said.

"We could try going around and sticking to the woods for some of the way, but sooner or later we'll have to step out into the open," Mom said, before glancing down at her feet. "Unfortunately, my shoes aren't well suited for that plan."

"I'm a cat, so it sounds to me like you are both stomping around like elephants anyway."

"Well, I've got an idea." I looked out over the lapping waves of the nearby lake. "I can provide cover all the way, no traipsing through the woods needed."

I reached out with my arcane senses and muttered the words of power to unlock the magic. My magic encouraged the warmer air higher above the lake to invert, dropping to the water's surface.

Warm, moist air blowing over cold water equals fog. Soon I had a nice, billowy fog bank, a veritable tsunami. I moved it from the lake onto the land, obscuring the estate from our view.

"Okay, that won't last long. We'd better get moving."

"How are we going to know which way to go if we can't see?" Selene demanded.

"Just take a page out of Dorothy's book and follow the brick road," I said. "And keep your voice down. The fog hides us from sight, but it doesn't obscure sound."

We crept through the fog, using the road to guide us right to the manor house. I kept my gaze swiveling about, looking for any sign of movement. I couldn't find any. I didn't see evidence of a vehicle either, so perhaps our intruder had come in from a different way. Then again, maybe this was all for nothing, and whoever was here had access to the massive garage.

For a time, the only sound was my own breathing and the occasional scuffle of shoes on pavement. The fog left a damp sheen on top of my skin, making my clothes cling to my body like a thick sheet.

I felt a growing trepidation in my belly, a gnawing sensation that something was not right. As our footfalls echoed out softly across the fog-covered ground, I got the impression that we weren't alone.

"Ssst," I said, grasping my mother's sleeve and dragging her to a halt.

I strained my ears, listening intently, but couldn't detect the underlying sound anymore.

I used my fingers to make a walking motion but placed a finger against my own lips with my other hand. Realization dawned in my mother's eyes, and she nodded. We continued on a short way, straining our ears to hear what was going on behind us. Then, I heard it, faint but definite: the scrape of a boot on the ground.

Mom withdrew a wand from inside her coat and mouthed a short incantation. A high-pitched chime rang out, like the single *ping* of a fork tapping a champagne flute, and a pressure coursed through the fog, while leaving the precipitation undisturbed.

"There," Mom spoke, still keeping her voice low, "we have two minutes where no one can hear us."

"Cone of silence spell?" Selene said, her tone clearly impressed.

Mom smiled. The spell had created a ten-foot circle around us where no sound would escape. In other words, we could hear whoever was stalking us, but they couldn't hear us.

"Something's following us," I said in a normal tone.

"You think?" Selene snapped. "What is it? The intruder?"

"I don't think so," I said, shaking my head. "Take a look at the fog bank I summoned."

Selene gazed around. "Yeah, what about it? It's getting thicker, so you might want to lay off."

"That's just it, Selene. I *did* lay off, quite a while ago. The fog should be growing thinner as time passes. Instead, it's growing thicker."

"So that means what, exactly?" Mom asked.

"I think I may have accidentally created the ideal environment for a Fog Wraith."

Mom's brows lifted. "Oh dear."

"Good work, Cora. A Fog Wraith. Just what we needed to liven this party up," Selene muttered.

"Hey, it's not like I sent it an engraved invitation, all right? Lay off."

Selene's whiskers twitched. "Uh, yeah, you kind of did. We should have just taken the bear spray and bull-rushed the place."

"Tick tock," Mom said.

Selene sighed. "Lavender used to go on and on about Fog Wraiths. Apparently, they inspired the Jack the Ripper legend, and are the reason why nobody goes for a walk on a foggy night in London."

"What can we do?" Mom asked. "Combat spells aren't my forte."

I swallowed hard. They weren't mine either.

For a moment, we all paused and held our breath, ears cocked. "It stopped moving," I said, keeping my voice low just in case. "They're not smart, but they have a kind of low cunning, like a predatory animal. They try to match their footsteps to those of their prey, slowly drawing nearer until it's time to strike."

"Well, I don't see anything." Selene peered about. "But it's getting so thick, I can barely see you two now."

"You're not likely to, until it's time for them to strike," I said miserably. "Fog Wraiths remain invisible most of the time, indistinct from the fog surrounding them."

"All right, well then you'd better use your wind magic and blow this stuff out of here. Take the nasty wraith with it."

"I can try, but if it doesn't work, and it just clears the fog, the wraith will have a line of sight on us. Just one touch from their wispy tendrils can rob you of years of life. That's if they're hungry. If, on the other hand, they're just bored, they'll kill you slowly with a corporeal blade, dragging out the agony as long as possible."

"Huh. Well, then I guess you two should run," Selene said. "If that's all it can do, I'm good."

"Selene—" I started, then quickly dropped it. Now wasn't the time to quarrel with her over her fairy tale about being the next-best thing to immortal.

"Did Aunt Lavender even say how to defeat one?" I asked, changing tactics.

"The silence spell is fading," Mom said, glancing around nervously.

"Uh, it boils down to don't get close to one in the first place," Selene replied.

"Great." I chewed the corner of my lip and glanced around. The fog was so thick, I was beginning to feel like some kind of amphibian, breathing in both air and water.

"If it wants a chase, then we'll give it one," I whispered, quickly kicking out of my white sneakers. "Mom, shoes off."

I quickly explained my plan, and in the final moments of the silence spell, Mom and I joined hands and created a new spell that animated both pairs of shoes, lifting them in a slow gait, as though disembodied feet resided within them. I set the shoes on a course toward the dark woods and waited.

Sure enough, I saw a wispy form drift along out of the fog less than twenty feet from us. I held my breath, watching as the wraith followed our decoy shoes. Only when it was well out of sight did I let go of the breath I'd been holding.

"Okay, I think we're safe. The shoes should keep going until they get snagged on something, and the wraith won't be able to follow once it reaches the edge of the fog. It should fade once the fog lifts. Although we should probably tell someone with the Magical Creature Containment unit that there's a Fog Wraith in Winterspell." I shuddered as the adrenaline receded.

We moved quietly as we continued up Salvatore's driveway, only taking a full sigh of relief once we were clear of the fog entirely. The relief was short lived though, as I paused at the corner of the garage and pointed at the darkened house. "Look. Do you see what I see?"

"A child, a child, shivers in the cold, let us bring him silver and gold—"

I shot the cat a dark look.

Mom craned her neck and then nodded. "I see it."

An unmistakable yellow bobbing light moved

about on the second floor. A flashlight wielded by an unseen intruder.

"How are we going to play this?" I asked. "Should we call the police?"

"For what, trespassing?" Selene asked. "Uh, hello, we're doing the same thing! Besides, that ward I set on the property wasn't strictly legal, if you get into the nitty-gritty of the magic code. Since you don't own this property, you don't have the right to use wards like that."

"Then it's a good thing I *didn't*," I growled.

"Technically speaking, you did," Selene replied, not even having the decency to look the least bit sheepish.

Mom pursed her lips thoughtfully. "You're sure this has something to do with Lavender?"

"Well, no. Not one hundred percent, but there's a good chance," I stammered. "But for all we know, this person works for the police department, and they just triggered Selene's secondhand spell through dumb luck."

"Way to throw me under the bus, Cora."

"You threw yourself under the bus the moment you decided to use me like some kind of tool. I'm going to have a hard time forgiving you for this one."

The cat looked unbothered. "Based on your

track record, it won't take long for you to get over it. I've done plenty worse that you don't even know about."

I sighed. "As if I needed paranoia on top of all my other problems, Selene."

I looked up at the bobbing light as it moved down the second-story hallway. It turned a corner and vanished.

"Tell me this, Miss Smarty Pants," Selene said. "If this intruder works for the police, how come they're tooling around in the dark with a flashlight instead of just hitting the light switch?"

"She has a point, Cora," Mother interjected.

"I don't know," I said with an exasperated exhale. "That's what they do on *CSI*."

"Sweet Mother, help us," Selene muttered. "You know those shows are about as realistic as the rack on a Victoria's Secret model, right?"

I cringed. "Selene, please, for the love of Mother Nature herself, *shut up!*"

"All right, all right, so it's highly unlikely they work for the cops. I just think we need to be careful. Remember how much trouble a fairly minor witch gave us last time? I don't want this case to be my last."

"All right, let's go inside and see what's going on.

But we need to be smart about it. We don't know what they're capable of."

"Well, darn," Selene said, her tone even thicker with sarcasm. "That just blew my whole plan out of the water. I thought that after all of the skulking around in the fog, we'd just bust in like the Kool-Aid man and shout, 'Hey, intruder, grab onto your keister because we're about to kick it.'"

Mom stared down at the pint-sized feline.

"Now you know what I've been dealing with," I told her. "Count your blessings that she had to go down to the next generational branch in the family tree, because otherwise, she'd be your problem."

"All right, enough talk," Selene snapped.

The cat sprinted across the driveway and up the handful of steps to the front door. She regarded it for a moment, her tail twitching like mad. "Hey, I think it's open just a crack. I bet I can just …"

"Selene, don't do it!" I hissed. "We have no idea if the intruder set any traps or—"

Selene vanished inside the house, and I clenched my teeth in frustration. Mom patted my shoulder with sympathy. "Next time, try telling her the oppo-site of what you want her to do. You never know, it might work."

18

I followed Selene inside, catching a flash of gray fur as she skittered up the grand staircase of Salvatore Greco's manor house. I moved a bit more cautiously, still not wanting to give myself away with heavy footsteps. Mom followed a few steps behind me, using the tip of her wand as a thin flashlight beam to light our way as we trailed Selene up the steps to the second floor. I glanced in the open door of Salvatore's study but saw nothing amiss. We continued on, passing half a dozen rooms I'd not seen on my previous visit.

I poked my head into one room and found its walls to be lined with Roman-style statuary. I figured it would be a good place to hide, so I diverged course into the room and peered about.

The statues were interesting but held no intruders hiding behind them. One statue depicted a Roman general astride a great warhorse, his sword drawn and held high. It was roughly proportional to a real man and horse and must have weighed a ton. Adjacent to the general statue, a pair of seminude lovers clasped in an embrace. Apollo and Daphne, the inscription read.

I moved around the room, seeing statues featuring Greek heroes and a pair of children nursing from a wolf mother. No sign of anyone else though, so I left the statue room and met up with my mother in the hall.

"Did you find anything?" I whispered.

"No," she replied, shaking her head. "I was in a room full of potions, though. Some of them are pretty expensive. If it's a thief, they're ignoring good merchandise."

I frowned and looked about in the darkness for Selene. "Now where did that cat get off to?"

"I don't know. I haven't seen her in a while—what was that?"

We both jolted at the muffled thud over our heads, like the sound of a heavy object falling and landing on a rug or thick carpeting. Mom raised her wand but dimmed her own light a little as we crept forward, our eyes peeled and ears strained. The yellow bobbing glow of the flashlight returned, coming down the staircase leading to the third floor. My mother and I nodded to each other and adopted positions on opposite sides of the wide hallway, using suits of armor as cover. Mom extinguished her own light, and I said a silent prayer, hoping wherever Selene was, she had enough sense to stay hidden.

My heart thudded in my chest as the light grew brighter. I swallowed hard and tried not to even breathe lest I give my position away. Whoever it was, they were in a hurry, muttering to themselves in a whisper as their footsteps quickened.

At last, the intruder walked past us, and I couldn't stifle a gasp of surprise.

"Michelle?" I blurted.

The woman yelped and stumbled back a few steps. She dropped what she was carrying and clutched at her chest, her face a mask of fear.

"What the—who are you and what are you doing here?" She narrowed her eyes and dropped her hand. "Wait! I know you. You came to my house, nosing around about Salvatore."

"What are you doing here, Michelle?" I asked, casting my own source of light overhead. I looked down at what she'd been lugging along: two full suitcases corralled together with a bungie cord, stuffed to the point that the soft sides were bulging.

"I'm just, um, cleaning up," Michelle said. "I have every right to be here for that purpose."

"Then why are you doing it in the dark? Skulking around like a thief?" I gestured at the suitcases. "What's in there? Your cleaning supplies, I suppose?"

Michelle cringed, glancing down at the suitcases. "Um, yes. That's right. Cleaning supplies. I'm getting the house ready for a showing now that we're putting it on the market."

I gave her flashlight a pointed look.

She followed my gaze. "The electricity has been cut off. A mix up with the power company, I suppose."

Mom reached over and flicked a light switch, and suddenly the hall was bathed in soft yellow light.

I quirked an eyebrow at Michelle.

She barely contained the beginning of a snarl. "Well, then a power fuse must be tripped, because the downstairs ones wouldn't turn on when I first got here. If anyone should be explaining themselves, it's you two! I was Salvatore's family; I have every right to be here in his house. You two are trespassing!"

While Michelle ranted, I sent a twirl of magic toward the suitcases and released the bungee cord. The suitcases spilled apart, and the zipper on the left one tore under the pressure, sending a cascade of hardback books spilling out the side.

"Interesting cleaning supplies," I said. "Looks to me more like you're stealing from Sal's estate."

"How dare you!" Michelle exclaimed. "That's it. I'm calling the police. You should go. Get a head start."

Selene trotted down the hall and came to stand between me and my mother. "Cracked the case, have you?" she asked. "I suppose we should have known it was you after you sent us on a goose chase to try and pin Sal's death on August Nell. Bet you figured we'd get slapped with a restraining order and drop the whole thing."

"I have no idea what you're talking about," Michelle said, though her voice wavered ever so slightly. "Salvatore left his library to me and Ernesto. I'm only taking what's mine."

"Not from what we heard," I replied, crossing my arms. "Those books were supposed to be donated to the library. And again, if they belong to you, why sneak them out in suitcases in the dark?"

"I—I told you—the lights are—" Michelle's face

screwed up with twisted rage. "Oh, never mind. Get out of my way!"

She tried to get past us, with her intact case full of books, but we didn't budge. "Interesting thing about the night Salvatore was killed," I said. "The police found a tumbler of bourbon sitting out on his desk."

Sweat broke out on Michelle's forehead. "W-what's that got to do with me?"

"It's just interesting because Salvatore never drank. His body couldn't handle it any longer. Most of the liquor on his shelf was unopened."

"That's fascinating, but it has nothing to do with me, personally. Now if you'll excuse me—"

"Someone wanted to make it look like Sal got drunk and fell down the stairs, but that was actually their mistake. Those in Sal's inner circle would know he didn't drink. He might have been your husband's uncle, but you didn't know him all that well, did you, Michelle?"

Michelle's eyes narrowed to slits. "Everyone makes mistakes. No one is perfect. Sal just slipped up."

"I don't think he did. Someone was here that night. They were rummaging around in his office, looking for something … maybe a specific book?" I dropped my gaze to the suitcase in her hand.

"What are you really doing with the books, Michelle? Planning to sell them off to your buddy, August, and use the profit to buy a one-way ticket away from your deadbeat husband?"

Michelle's jaw flexed as she glared at the cat.

"Don't pretend to be upset, Michelle," Selene continued. "We know how you really feel about him. He's an embarrassment. Always getting up to drunk shenanigans, which you then have to clean up, all the while taking care of him and his needs. It's enough to drive anyone up the wall."

"What does my relationship with my husband have to do with anything?" Michelle spat. "Now, excuse me, I really do need to get these books down to storage. It's getting late."

"Oh, and where will they be stored at?" I asked.

Her mouth twisted into a scowl. "At a storage unit downtown, of course."

"The one that sits across the street from the marina?" I asked.

"Yes, that one."

"Funny, there's no storage unit place anywhere near the marina," Mom said with a frown.

"Who cares where I'm going to take them? Now

for the last time, get out of my way." Michelle's eyes shone with fury. "I'm not going to ask you again."

"She seems pretty angry." Selene looked up at me. "You think she got this angry on the night that she pushed Sal down the stairs?"

"Shut up!" Michelle snapped.

"She clearly has anger management issues—"

"Tell that cat to shut up! I do not have issues!" Michelle growled.

"Maybe we should call Ernesto and see what he's got to say about this storage unit business," I suggested.

"No!" Michelle's eyes flashed red, and the suits of armor began to rattle and shake. Her lips muttered a spell, and I knew that it was about to hit the fan.

"Everybody down!" I shouted, dragging Mom down to the floor, almost crushing Selene beneath us. Michelle finished chanting, and a white marble fist smashed through the drywall where our heads had been a few moments before.

"You can't have these books!" Michelle howled as the animated statue of the Roman soldier tore through the wall with its marble fingers. "I've earned these books. All of the garbage Ernesto has put me through—" she scoffed. "These books are my ticket to a new life."

We scrambled back, farther down the hallway, as the statue finished demolishing the wall. It stood protectively in front of Michelle, sword held at the ready.

"What makes you think you deserve a new life?" Selene shouted.

"Ernesto wasn't always a drunk disgrace with a permanent coating of cheese puff dust and potato chip grease," Michelle snarled. "He was supposed to *be* something. He had all the money and opportunities in the world back when we met."

Michelle gave an angry toss of her head before sending her statue-turned-bodyguard marching down the hall toward us. "I'm simply taking what should have been mine from the start," she snapped. "I've put in the time. I've been the doting wife. I earned it with all the times I cleaned up his messes, and the times I had to drive to the police station in the middle of the night to bail him out of the drunk tank. This is for all of the times I had to endure the snickers and scoffs of people who thought they were better than me because their husbands weren't lazy slobs."

"Why not just ask Sal for help?" I asked, still retreating carefully to the staircase. The statue moved slowly but we would be out of room soon.

"He loved Ernesto like a son. He named him as his successor to his cushy jobs. You've hung on this long; why not wait a little longer and get the big payday?"

Michelle barked a hollow laugh. "Oh, yeah. For a week, a month at best, and then Ernesto would find some way to squander that job, too. As for Sal, he didn't believe me. Ernesto was his golden boy. He overlooked all of his flaws."

She dragged her suitcase behind her as she followed the menacing Roman soldier down the hall, using him as cover. "You don't know what it's like! You don't have a clue what it's like to hit the end of your rope. I didn't have a choice."

"So, you admit it then? You came here to ask for help and when Sal wouldn't give it, you shoved him down the stairs?"

Michelle stopped walking. Her eyes darted from me to the statue, then back again. Something shifted and her expression turned haunted. "I didn't mean for him to get hurt. All I wanted was for him to listen to me. To take me seriously for once. I never wanted anybody to die, I—"

My breath caught in my throat. I had Michelle hooked, and I wanted to keep her talking.

"I just couldn't take it anymore," she said, her

voice thick. "I couldn't take being the laughingstock. All I wanted was to be free. To not have to work three times as hard as everyone else just to keep things from crumbling."

She stopped and so did her marble sentinel. Her grip on the magic must have slipped. "I—I only went to see Salvatore that night to convince him to see reason. All I wanted was one book. I'd spoken with August at the charity dinner, and he'd told me how much he was willing to pay for it. I got so angry at Sal for—for everything. I work two jobs just to keep the house, and when I come home from work, I have to do the cooking and cleaning and landscaping, because lord knows we can't afford to hire help. Not anymore."

Her face twisted with a fresh wave of bitterness. "Salvatore could have written a check and paid the balance of our mortgage without even noticing that money had left his account. He was *that* wealthy. Still, he wanted to play games with some rich guys just for kicks, knowing full well that was life-changing money."

"Did he know how much trouble you were in?" I asked, suddenly confused. If Sal loved Ernesto like his own blood, how could he stand by and watch him and his wife struggle when he could easily solve it? Something wasn't adding up.

"Ernesto was too proud to beg," Michelle said with a shake of her head. "Besides, Sal had just named Ernesto as his successor to his place on the board and with the Arcane Council. As you said, that payday would have changed things for us. He probably figured that he'd done enough. Sal knew Ernesto had lost jobs in the past, but he didn't know the full extent of his drinking problem. He didn't know about the DUIs or the drunk and disorderly charges over the years. Ernesto swore me to secrecy."

"So, when you came here that night, you were going to spill the beans?" I asked.

Nodding, she covered her face with her hands and sobbed. "I told him everything and asked him for the book August wanted. That's all I wanted. Just one stupid little book." Michelle sniffed and wiped her eyes, smearing her mascara over her cheekbones. "But Salvatore refused. He told me to be grateful for everything he'd already done. I started crying, and he got nasty with me, and told me that I should try harder to live within my means. So, I was standing here, in this ridiculous house, practically drowning in all his displays of wealth, while he asked me if I knew how to use coupons at the market, and I just, I just …"

"You just what, Michelle?" I prompted in a soft tone.

"I snapped." Her eyes widened. "I shoved him. Really hard. I wanted him to shut up, to stop talking and sneering at me—but he tripped on the carpet and—" She paused and squeezed her eyes shut tight. "His head made this … *awful* noise when he hit the bottom of the stairs, and I just knew—I knew it was too late."

She looked down at the very carpet runner that led to Sal's demise. "I panicked. He wasn't breathing. There was nothing I could do to take it back, so I—I staged the scene with the liquor. I had to make it look like an accident. Then I went looking for the book, but I got spooked when a car pulled into the drive, and I bolted."

"Who was in the car?"

Michelle frowned. "It was just someone using the driveway to turn around, but I'd already lost my nerve. I couldn't bring myself to go back inside and see him … like that."

Michelle's gaze snapped back to us, and the present. Rage boiled in her eyes, and I remembered that accident or not, this woman had killed a man just a few days before. "And everything would have been fine if you two hadn't interfered! Why couldn't you just leave well enough alone? I still have no idea how any of this matters to you? What are you, just a couple of bored citizen detectives?" Her sneer sharpened. "You should have joined a Bunco club instead."

Shifting her eyes to the immobile statue, she raised her free hand and spoke a single command word. The statue lurched forward, swinging its sword. Mom tried to duck, getting out of reach of the bladed edge, but she wasn't quick enough. The hilt of the sword connected with her chest, knocking her prone to the floor.

"Mom!" In a panic, I scrambled back and summoned a gust of wind to blast the statue back, but it was no use. The thing was too heavy and strong. The mass of sculpted marble cut through the cyclone without even a split second of hesitation.

A *crack* sounded and a blast of pink sparks blasted through the hall. Selene's signature calling card. The cat's magic was limited, but she knew way more spells than I did, and apparently had landed on one with enough firepower to blast a chunk of marble off the soldier's arm.

Another *crack* followed and she managed to snap through the arm entirely. While she was keeping

Michelle and the statue occupied, I raced over to my mother. "Mom, are you all right?"

"I think so," she muttered, her face a mask of pain as she struggled to her feet, one hand pressed to her chest where the stone had connected.

"We need to get you to a hospital," I said, trying to help my mother to stand. Twisting around, I saw the hallway behind the statue was empty aside from the suitcases of books. "She got away!" I cried.

"Think again!" Michelle's voice said, coming from behind the struggling statue as Selene continued hammering away at it with her blasts of magic.

Michelle cast a ball of something dark, scream-ing, and nasty at me. I had no idea what kind of spell —or creature—it was, nor did I know how to counter it.

Everything seemed to slow down as the green, hissing ball burned down the hallway toward me and my mother. "Selene! Use me! I give my permission."

A rush of magic jolted through my body, hot and fast, like wild horses running across the high desert.

A spell flashed through my mind, its words foreign, but there wasn't time to question it. I spoke them loudly and let Selene's spell move through me until it released with a *whoosh* so powerful it shoved back against me on the way out of my hands, like the kickback of a shotgun.

The screeching ball of magic bowled toward us, singeing the paint off the walls as it went.

A silver and purple form that looked suspiciously like a certain cat flew into the air to meet the ball. Shadow Selene was enveloped in an ivory glow midair and used a paw to bat away the demonic fireball like she was returning a tennis serve.

Michelle shrieked as her missile tore back toward her.

An explosion of light, sound, and fragments of marble statue shattered the hallway and turned it into abject chaos personified. I wondered if we were still alive.

19

I rolled onto my stomach and shook my head, a pervasive ringing all I could hear. Everything seemed too bright, and my head ached from the awful ringing. Once, when I was a child, I'd done a belly flop off a diving board into a pool. The resulting molecular ache felt quite similar to what I experienced as I came to on the floor of Salvatore Greco's lakeside estate.

I grew dimly aware of someone's voice, but I couldn't make out the words. All I could hear was the ringing, and a muffled underlay beneath it. I felt a hand on my shoulder, which seemed to sort of ground me back in reality.

"Mom?" I knew I spoke. I felt my throat vibrate, moved my lips and tongue, and yet I didn't hear a sound. I looked up, squinting in the bright light as my mother put her hand on my temple and chanted a spell.

I gasped as the ringing subsided, and the lights seemed to dim. I steadied myself with a hand against the wall and shook my head.

"What happened?"

"I—I'm not sure, but it looked like Selene, or a phantom of Selene, bounced Michelle's spell back at her, and there was an explosion when the magical energy fields collided. The transmutation magic it took to animate the statue was like antimatter to the demonic energy of her final attack."

"Michelle and her little friend went ka-pow," Selene said, licking her paw. "To put it somewhat more succinctly."

"Are you okay?" I asked both of them.

"Naturally," Selene replied before arching into a long stretch.

Mom nodded. "I'm all right."

Blinking, I looked about the marble strewn floor, and saw only fragments of statue and plaster. I did not see Michelle anywhere. "Where did Michelle go? Is she ... did she...?"

"She's very much alive, but when she wakes up, she's probably not going to want to be." Selene trotted down to the end of the hall and jumped up onto the large windowsill, mindful of the broken glass scattered about. "Take a gander out in the backyard."

I got to my feet and picked my way through the wreckage to peer out the window. "Mother, Maiden, Crone," I whispered.

Michelle had been blasted clean out the second-story window and fallen into the thick perimeter of hedges below. One of her legs was bent at an unnatural angle, but she was starting to stir awake.

"We need to call for a healer," I said, backing away from the window. "She needs help."

"Yes, of course, dear, help is on the way. Along with Sheriff Templeton."

I rubbed my head. "How long was I out?"

"A minute, maybe two," Selene said casually as she kept watch out the window. "Lilac and I had the good sense to hit the deck. You're the one who stood there and let the shockwave blow you over."

Mom placed a soothing hand on my back. "I think you have a mild concussion, dear, but a little bit of healing magic will have you right as rain."

"I for one can't wait to see Sheriff Templeton's face when we tell him we've solved our *second* murder investigation while he's had his rotund keister glued to a bar stool," Selene said, her eyes glowing with delight.

"Oh, believe me, he's going to get an earful from me, too," Mom said, shaking her head. "Samuel needs a wake-up call, and I'm going to give it to him. We went to school together, you know."

"You did? I had no idea. He looks so much older than you," I told my mom.

She beamed and reached up to run her fingers through her tousled hair. "Why thank you, dear."

We moved to the ground floor and awaited Templeton's arrival. He came screeching up the private drive a few minutes later, an ambulance and several deputies in tow.

I don't know if it was my mother's presence or what, but he seemed on better behavior as we gave him the rundown of our encounter with Michelle. Granted, he kept a sour look on his face as he grunted along.

"I should run you all in for interfering with a criminal investigation," he said when we finished.

"You've got to be kidding, Samuel!" Mom got right up in his mustachioed face. "Cora and Selene did all of the hard work and wrapped up this case in a bow before serving you the perp on a silver platter.

You should be thanking them, not threatening them!"

"I don't know about all of that, Lilac. This so-called confession is hearsay at best in a court of law. So, unless one of you happened to get it on tape, I'm not sure how much use it will be, and now that you've knocked her half-unconscious, I doubt she'll be in a mood to talk once we read her her rights."

Templeton shook his head, his bushy mustache twitching. "You'd better hope we can gather enough physical evidence to make the charges stick."

Mom sighed as Templeton shuffled off to speak with his deputies. "That man just doesn't know how to say the words thank you."

"He's under a curse where if he utters the words thank you, he'll choke to death on his own bile."

"Really?" I asked, turning to Selene.

"Naw, he's just a jerk. Pretty cool explanation, though, right? I bet I could be a writer on a TV show. Selene Productions. No, Productions by Selene. I like the sound of that!"

"Don't quit your day job."

Mom drove us to my house. The healers at Sal's house had checked all of us over and worked their magic on our injuries. We'd likely feel it in the morning, but for now, we were all okay.

"Are you sure you don't want to stay with me tonight?" Mom asked as she pulled into my driveway. "I have the guest room already made up."

"It's okay, Mom. I want to sleep in my own bed tonight. But I promise I'll call in the morning, okay?"

Mom nodded. "Okay. Sweet dreams, both of you."

I doubted that was possible, but I didn't want to burst her bubble, so I smiled, kissed her on the cheek, and scurried inside with Selene hot on my heels.

"What a night," I sighed as we shuffled through the door. "At least the shop is already closed tomorrow, because there's no way I'm doing *anything* tomorrow."

"Me either," Selene agreed, already marching into the kitchen.

I tossed my keys into the bowl on the table beside the door and smiled. I already knew what she wanted. Even after all of that excitement, all Selene could focus on was her next meal.

"Is it weird that I'm relieved Michelle is all right, even after she tried to kill us?" I asked as I dished out Selene's overpriced cat food.

"Very," she replied.

I sighed. "Never mind. I guess I just feel bad for her."

"Why?"

"It's just that … well, I know how much your life can change from the way you planned it. It's not easy to come to grips with watching your dreams die."

"Oh, spare me. You're divorced and a little bit sad about it. You didn't go on a killing spree just because you were upset your marriage ended. Michelle had options; she chose not to take them."

I set Selene's bowl on the floor and had to admit she was right. The only thing I'd killed after my life crumbled was a case or two of chardonnay.

"I swear, you hairless apes get all bent out of shape over the silliest things," Selene said in between bites. "You should try curling up and taking a nap in a patch of sunlight. It's like chicken soup that you absorb through your skin."

I laughed. "After the night that I had, curling up into a ball and sleeping sounds like a wonderful idea."

A pair of headlights flashed through the front window, and I frowned. "That better not be Sheriff Templeton coming to pepper us with a bunch of questions," I muttered, already going for the front door.

"Or to arrest us," Selene called after me.

"Yeah, or that."

I peeked out the window and my heart warmed when I recognized the vehicle parked behind my car. It was Clint's BMW. With a smile, I tugged open the front door and greeted him before his shiny loafers even reached the front porch.

He wore a nice suit, but his necktie had been loosened at some point during the course of the day. He looked a little disheveled, which actually surprised me. "Hi, Clint? Is everything all right?"

He came up to join me on the porch. "I came here to ask you the same thing," he said.

I frowned. "What do you mean?"

Had he somehow heard about what happened at Sal's? There was no way.

"I've been trying to reach you all night, but you've been sending me straight to voicemail. Listen, Cora, I'm sorry if I spooked you with talk about staying in town long-term, but I—"

"Wait, hold on. What are you talking about? I didn't get any calls." I dug into my pocket and found my phone. I tapped the screen and nothing happened. "Shoot, looks like my battery died. I'm really sorry. I didn't mean to make you think I'd ghosted you."

Relief flooded Clint's eyes as he looked down at his shoes and chuckled. He raked a hand through his hair. "Geeze, I am really making an idiot of myself here, aren't I?"

"Yep!" Selene chimed in as she stepped out onto the porch between us, still licking her whiskers clean.

He laughed. "Thanks for always keeping it real, Selene."

"Come inside," I told him. "We have a lot to catch you up on."

He cocked an eyebrow. "What happened?"

We stepped into the living room and Clint frowned at me as he reached over and plucked a bit of white from my hair. "What the— is this plaster?"

"Marble, actually. Or maybe bits of drywall." I chuckled. "I guess it's kind of a bad sign that I don't know which one it is."

Selene and I recapped the night's events, not skimping on any details. Clint listened intently with an increasing look of horror on his face.

"Are you sure you're all right?" he asked when I finished, his eyes roving over me looking for signs of injury. When he was sure I wasn't hurt, he gathered me in a near rib-crushing embrace. "You could have been killed!"

I smiled into his chest and melted into the warm embrace, quite content to stay there for the foreseeable future. "I swear I'm fine. Just really tired."

He pulled back, only far enough to look down into my eyes, his artfully manicured brows coming low over his eyes, making them seem hooded. "I wish you would have called me to come with you. I don't mean that to sound all caveman, you know, me strong man, you little woman, but—"

Selene cackled.

Clint ran the pad of his thumb over my cheek. "Cora, I'd be devastated if anything happened to you. You mean a lot to me."

My heart swelled and for a moment we stood suspended in time, our eyes locked.

"Ugh. If you two are gonna get all mushy, I'm out of here," Selene groused, turning around to retreat to the kitchen.

Clint smiled. "I guess now we know how to get rid of her."

"I *heard* that!" Selene called from around the corner.

I laughed softly and popped up onto my tiptoes to kiss Clint. "I'm sorry I missed your calls, and you're probably right. The whole thing was reckless. I swear I'm not normally like this. It's just—well, this is about family. It's like I have blinders on when it comes to anything to do with my aunt. And after my mom told us about what she heard through the scrying mirror—" I paused as a wave of emotions rolled over me. "I got desperate. Maybe a little crazy."

"I understand," he said, taking both of my hands into his. He squeezed them gently. "I admire your tenacity and determination. Your loyalty."

I smiled. "I'm glad you're here. Do you think you could stay? I'd sleep better knowing you're next to me."

He pulled me into his chest again. "Anything you want."

It was odd, how the chaos and danger melted away as I stood there in Clint's arms. They say the universe works in mysterious ways, and I was beginning to wonder if maybe the universe had placed Clint in my path at just the right moment after all.

"Are you hungry?" Clint asked after a long moment. "I'm not much of a chef, but I can make you an omelet if you want?"

"An omelet sounds perfect," I told him.

He took my hand and led me into the kitchen and instructed me to sit and let him handle everything. As he pulled open cupboards and drawers looking for supplies, he smiled over at me. "My day wasn't nearly as exciting as yours, but I do have a bit of news to share."

"Oh yeah?"

He located a mixing bowl and pulled it down from the cabinet. "I signed a lease on a house just a couple of neighborhoods over from here. It's six months to start, but it has an option to extend, if … well, if that works out."

My heart fluttered and I beamed at him.

Something told me that it would.

Thank you, universe.

20

We had solved the mystery of who killed the legendary archivist, Salvatore Greco. Unfortunately, that still left us the first mystery: Who had taken Aunt Lavender? And where were they keeping her?

Michelle's confession, while colorful, hadn't provided any further clues, and in the aftermath, I wondered if the line I'd drawn from Salvatore to Lavender was all in my head.

A few days after Michelle's arrest, my mom went to speak with Sheriff Templeton in private. She called me afterward and told me she'd convinced the sheriff to redouble his efforts to help us find Lavender. He dispatched deputies to ask around her neighborhood, to see if anyone could recall seeing strange activity around Lavender's house over the weeks leading up to her abduction. I wasn't sure it would turn up any new leads, but it was encouraging that at least something was being done.

Selene, Clint, and I spent most of our evenings at the library. We developed a system of sorts. During the day, my mom and Selene would research in the library while I worked at Wicked Wicks. When I closed up shop, I would then go and "tag in," taking my shift while Mom went home to rest. Oftentimes, Clint would show up before closing time and help me recover the shop. Then we would head over to the library together after picking up a quick bite.

One night, about a week after the confrontation with Michelle, Frankie approached us and confirmed that the *Odyssey of Obin Amorath* was not among the books donated on behalf of Sal's estate. She also told us that she closely followed rare book circles and hadn't heard any chatter about someone gaining possession of it. It appeared that Sal had kept news of the book a little quieter than we'd originally imagined.

I asked her what would happen to Ernesto's promotions, but she got tight-lipped and brushed it off, saying it wasn't her concern. Word around town was that Ernesto hadn't left the house since

Michelle's arrest. He hadn't even shown his face at Merlin's Well. I pitied the man. He'd lost his uncle and his wife all in the span of a week and a half. His entire life was inside out, and judging by what I knew of him, he wasn't equipped to handle the transition well.

As the days rolled by, the four of us developed an easy camaraderie, congratulating each other on every contribution to the effort no matter how minor, trying to keep our spirits high. Our problem seemed nearly insurmountable, however. We had no idea if Lavender had actually taken the book in the first place, and even if she had, how would anyone have known about it? She wasn't the type to go around bragging. So, either her abduction wasn't because of the book, which opened an endless can of worms, or Sal had ratted Lavender out and put a target on her back.

Of the two possibilities, the second seemed more likely. But Sal was gone now. We couldn't ask him who he'd told. Which led us back to Selene's method of reverse engineering our way to the answer. If we could figure out who was after Obin's treasures *and* had a connection to Sal, we just might find our perpetrator.

The only problem was that without the tome

itself, we had to rely on the research and information of others to narrow down our scope of targets. Eventually, we all focused in on our own personal theories. Mom thought she might be after the last remaining branch from the Tree of Life. I thought it might be something relating to the Fountain of Youth, seeing as Salvatore had mentioned that mystery himself during our brief chat. Clint, on the other hand, was struggling to keep up a doggy paddle in the flood of magical information we were throwing around. As someone who had spent most of his life in the non-magic world, he was a little like a kid in a chocolate factory. Or a monkey in space, as Selene put it.

For her part, Selene was insistent that Lavender was after something called the Archimedes Death Ray.

"I'm just saying, that if you're going for ancient weaponry, you might as well go big," she said as she argued her case.

Clint stared at her, his brow furrowed. "Really? I've never even heard of this ... Archimedes? Death Ray? That sounds like science fiction, doesn't it?"

"Oh good grief," I said, slurping on my iced coffee. "You've stepped in it now."

"You've never heard of Archimedes and his death

ray?" Selene spat. "You are such a peasant, aren't you? Didn't they teach you to read in that fancy human school of yours?"

"Selene ..." I warned.

"Ugh. All right, fine. Here are the highlights. Picture this, a whole mess of Romans were trying to conquer Archimedes' Greek friends, and the Greeks were like *Archie, baby, you've got to help us out. We can't fight all those Romans. We'll get our butts kicked.* So, Archimedes sits down to think about it for a while. This all happened on a scorching day, so he's sitting there, all thirsty and sweating, and gets the bright idea to use the sun's rays against his enemy."

"She isn't going to stop," I said politely to Clint.

"So, Archie gets a bunch of mirrors and straps them to this giant wooden frame of a horse, and they park it outside the city walls. I think there was a Medusa's head and a princess chained up for a sea monster snack in there somewhere too—anyway, the point is, the death ray worked like a charm, and totally burned the Roman fleet before they could even set foot on Greek soil. Archimedes was treated as a hero, but he feared his own creation and therefore launched it into outer space. It landed on the dark side of the moon, where it's been ever since. A giant horse covered with polished mirrors that reflect the sun's rays to deadly effect—"

"Mother, Maiden, and Crone," I muttered, setting aside my empty cup. "I think you're getting at least two or three different stories mixed up there. This is what I get for letting you watch *Troy* and *Clash of the Titans* in one weekend."

Mom perked up and fanned herself. "Whew, can we talk about how good Brad Pitt looked in that movie?"

"Um, absolutely not!" I squeaked.

"I should see about renting that one sometime soon. Get a nice bottle of wine and just—"

"Mom, I'm begging you. Please. Stop. Talking."

Mom giggled, her cheeks still flushed as she shifted her attention back to the open book in front of her.

"Even if there is a death ray, and I'm pretty sure there isn't, what would Lavender want with it? Also, didn't you just say it's on the moon—which, again, *it's not*, but seriously, Selene. Do you hear yourself right now?"

Clint lifted the cover of a heavy leather-bound volume. "And we're sure we ruled out the stake that was used to kill Count Dracula?"

"Lavender hates Eurotrash," Selene said.

"What about the Salt Shaker of Poseidon?" Mom asked, gesturing to a drawing in the book she had propped before her. "This says it works underwater."

Selene sighed and shook her head. "I don't think a waterproof salt shaker is worth the trouble of kidnapping an old witch."

"Well, then maybe we need to circle back to the original theory, that it's not about a specific item, but about the book itself. You heard what Michelle told us. It was worth a small fortune."

"Not as much as one of the treasures," Selene replied, her tone edgy. "Like the—"

I held up a hand. "If you say it one more time I'm going to scream."

"Hey, wait a minute," Clint said excitedly, his gaze glued to the pages of the book he was reading. "I think I may have found something."

With a warning glare shot Selene's way, I leaned over and peered at the book in his hands. "What is it?"

He pointed at a long list that spanned nearly the entirety of the two pages he was opened to. "See here? It's a list of treasures that have been found. Like a *Guinness Book of World Records*, only it relates solely to puzzles of Obin's treasure maps that have been solved."

"That is useful," I said, whistling. "Nice job, Clint."

He beamed me a smile, and I felt my heart quiver a little bit. Selene of course had to interrupt our sweet moment.

"Yeah, yeah, the sun shines on every dog's butt once in a while. Look and see if Archimedes' death ray has been found yet."

"It's not Archimedes' death ray!" Clint, Mom, and I shouted in unison.

A librarian gave us a dark stare from her perch at the check-out desk.

"Sorry," I called out softly. "You're going to get us kicked out, Selene!" I hissed at the cat.

"I wasn't the one shouting, *Cora*."

Ignoring her, I leaned in closer to Clint and ran my finger down the margin of the list. "All right, let's look at Poseidon's salt shaker. That seemed to be one we could all agree on."

Clint's face contorted into a frown as my finger stopped on the entry. "The salt shaker was found in 1934 and is on display at some museum back east."

"Well, that's a bust. What about the sword of Damascus?"

"Revealed to be a hoax in 1789."

"Darn it. The Ark of the Covenant?"

"Ditto, in 1981. Huh, that's funny. A year after the movie came out."

"What movie?" Selene asked.

"*Raiders of the Lost Ark.*" I rolled my eyes. "With Harrison Ford."

"Oh, that's one of those *Star Trek* ones, right? I love those. Frack it, I'm a Cylon! Everybody get back to the Firefly and ignite your Patronus charms!"

Clint frowned.

"Her attention span is really better suited for reality TV," I muttered. "Let's keep looking."

"Oh, wait. Here's a list of the quests they believe have yet to be solved," Clint said, flipping toward the back of the book. He read aloud, "*It is believed that the mysterious Golden Lotus brooch might hold the key to Obin Amorath's most ambitious—and most valuable—treasure yet. The brooch itself was recovered by a pair of treasure-seeking brothers in the early 1900s, and some say the brooch is cursed and drove the brothers to madness. Their father, a wealthy oil tycoon, took the brooch and had it severed into two halves, in an effort to end their warring. However, his plan backfired when his sons attacked him, resulting in his death. The brothers were executed for the murder of their father, and the brooch was lost. To this day, no one knows the location of either half of the Golden Lotus.*"

"So, wait, it just vanished? Does it say what the brooch does?" I asked.

Clint shook his head. "No, but if it was in the book, surely that explains its powers."

"We need to find that book," Selene said.

We fell silent for a long moment, then Mom perked up. "Have you checked anywhere outside Lavender's house?"

"No." I shook my head. "We've been more than busy enough with the insides. Why?"

Mom was already scrambling to her feet. "I think —I think I might know where she hid it."

I grabbed my coat and we raced out of the library to my car. We all but flew across town to Aunt Lavender's house. Mom burst out of the car and immediately went around the side of the house. Selene, Clint, and I all exchanged a look, then hurried to follow her.

Mom stopped at the base of the stairs leading to the kitchen door, then began pulling things from her coat pockets. Carefully, she placed a variety of crystals and stones in a circle around her feet, then straightened and closed her eyes. She spoke an incantation, and a pulse of magic surged from the collection of objects, forming a glowing blue line around her ankles. With another word, the spell shot out toward the trees at the back edge of Lavender's property and swirled around the trunk of a weeping willow in the corner.

"That one," Mom said, pointing at the tree when she opened her eyes. "Lavender always used to say that Mother Nature made for the best of secret keepers," she said as she marched across the yard toward the tree. When she reached it, the blue course of magic swept up the trunk and formed a rune before vanishing in a puff of magic smoke.

Mom spoke another spell and I blinked, unsure I believed my own eyes when that section of tree trunk opened as easily as a cupboard door and revealed a shelf full of books and what looked like an urn.

"Oh, that's where you ended up," Mom said, running her fingers over the silver urn. "It's good to see you, Mom."

"That's—that's Grandma Laurel?" I asked, an unexpected ball of emotion clogging my throat. She'd been gone for close to a decade now, but seeing her urn brought back childhood memories.

"Yes. Normally witches prefer their remains be returned to the Earth, dust to dust, and all that," Mom explained. "But your grandmother always did like to go against the grain. She asked that Lavender and I always keep her close. She couldn't bear the thought of being parted from her girls."

Mom removed the urn and handed it to me. "Here, we'll take her back to my place, until we bring Lavender back. All right?"

I took the urn and Mom swiped at her eyes before turning her attention to the other treasures stored in the tree trunk.

"I can't believe I didn't know Lavender was part Keebler elf," Selene said.

Mom laughed softly and ran her fingers along the books. With a soft gasp, she removed one from the shelf. "Here it is."

I almost lost my grip on my grandmother's urn.

"Oh, wow!" Clint breathed.

"We should get inside," I exclaimed, nervously glancing over my shoulder.

Mom closed the piece of tree trunk, broke the spell, and the bark melded back together without so much as a splinter to reveal we'd just cracked open a huge hole. I blinked a few times, still marveling at my aunt's handiwork.

We went inside and gathered around Lavender's dining table. Mom opened the book's cover and slowly flipped through the weathered pages, careful not to cause a crease or tear. We made it through the majority of the pages when we came to one with a watercolor-style painting of a yellow lotus flower.

Excitement swelled in my chest. "This is it!"

Mom turned the page, and we all recoiled.

The chunk of pages following the drawing had been torn out.

"You have *got* to be kidding me," Selene groaned. "What do we do now?"

Silence was the only answer any of us had to give.

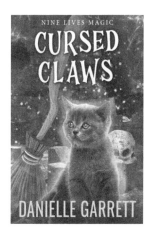

TRACKING down Aunt Lavender's kidnapper is proving to be more difficult than swimming through a pool filled with peanut butter. Every lead we uncover ends with more questions than answers.

We're running out of ideas—and time, too. The mysterious Golden Lotus seems to hold the key to the investigation, but no one can tell us what it does or why Aunt Lavender might have been looking for it.

And if that wasn't enough to keep both my cranky feline familiar and me completely occupied, we find ourselves thrust into the center of another criminal investigation—this time as the lead suspects.

We have to work together to clear our names and get the Winterspell PD off our tails so we can continue our hunt for Aunt Lavender and the mysterious Golden Lotus.

Time is burning faster than the wick on one of my enchanted candles, and I fear it's about to sputter out.

Order your copy today!

If you'd like to know what it was like when Selene first came to live with Cora, you can join my newsletter and receive a free copy of the short story, A Tail of Nine Lives Magic.
www.DanielleGarrettBooks.com/newsletter

If you'd like to chat with me on come join the Bat Wings Book Club on Facebook. It's my happy little corner of the internet and I love chatting with readers and sharing behind the scenes fun.

IF YOU'D LIKE to spend more time in Winterspell, check out the original series set in this magical town. Sprinkles and Sea Serpents is full of sweet treats, sassy cats, and a talking sea monster! *Find the Sugar Shack Witch Mysteries on Amazon.*

UNTIL NEXT TIME, **happy reading!**
Danielle Garrett
www.DanielleGarrettBooks.com

ALSO BY DANIELLE GARRETT

One town. Two spunky leading ladies.
More magic than you can shake a wand at.
Welcome to Beechwood Harbor.

Come join the fun in Beechwood Harbor, the little town where witches, shifters, ghosts, and vamps all live, work, play, and— mostly—get along!

The two main series set in this world are the Beechwood Harbor Magic Mysteries and the Beechwood Harbor Ghost Mysteries.

In the following pages you will find more information about those books, as well as my other works available.

Alternatively, you can find a complete reading list on my website:

www.DanielleGarrettBooks.com

In Winterspell Lake there are things darker than midnight...

Sprinkles and Sea Serpents is the first book in a brand new paranormal cozy mystery series by Danielle Garrett. This series features magic, mystery, family squabbles, sassy heroines, and a mysterious monster hunter—all with a little sugar sprinkled on top.

Find the Sugar Shack Witch Mysteries on Amazon.

ABOUT THE AUTHOR

Danielle Garrett has been an avid bookworm for as long as she can remember, immersing herself in the magic of far-off places and the rich lives of witches, wizards, princesses, elves, and some wonderful everyday heroes as well. Her love of reading naturally blossomed into a passion for storytelling, and today, she's living the dream she's nurtured since the second grade—crafting her own worlds and characters as an author.

A proud Oregonian, Danielle loves to travel but always finds her way back to the Pacific Northwest, where she shares her life with her husband and their beloved menagerie of animal companions.

Visit Danielle today at her website or say "hello" on Facebook.

www.DanielleGarrettBooks.com